Brianna was astonished by Philippe's accusation

"A girl's eyes," he said, "can incite a man to do anything. They're the most formidable weapon a woman can have; and you have singularly beautiful eyes, *mon ange.*"

Her color slowly deepened as they stared at each other. A tremor ran through her body and she held her breath as his arms reached out to take hold of her roughly and pull her toward him. He jerked her face up to his and pressed his lips against her mouth in a kiss that spread flames through every part of her being.

Why on earth had he kissed her? Merely to prove his point that a platonic friendship was impossible between a man and a woman? What did he really feel for Brianna Gaze?

OTHER
Harlequin Romances
by DOROTHY CORK

Forget and Forgive

by

DOROTHY CORK

Harlequin Books

TORONTO • LONDON • NEW YORK • AMSTERDAM
SYDNEY • HAMBURG • PARIS

Original hardcover edition published in 1978
by Mills & Boon Limited

ISBN 0-373-02242-5

Harlequin edition published March 1979

PRINTED IN U.S.A.

CHAPTER ONE

'YOU'RE crazy you know, Bri,' Peter Arden said.

He followed Brianna into the sitting room and switched on the lamp by the sofa, then sat down with the familiarity of one who was very much at home there. As he was, for he and Brianna Gaze had been good friends for two years now, and this was her house. Since her grandmother's death, six weeks ago, she had rented part of it to a married couple, but they had their own sitting room upstairs and Brianna could still entertain privately.

She stood looking at him for a moment, her hazel eyes, where gold vied with grey for supremacy, wide and direct, her almost straight, light brown hair shining in the lamplight.

'Why am I crazy?' she asked finally, and sat, not on the sofa beside Peter, but in an armchair facing him.

'You know perfectly well why. Haring off across the Channel to fling yourself into the midst of a family of—frogs, when I've heard you say a million times that the only real family you ever had is here in Canterbury.'

'Yes—but there's no one left now, since Gran died,' Brianna said. 'And when you talk about "frogs", Peter—just don't forget my mother is French!'

'Sorry. But I do forget—all the time. There's nothing Gallic about you. You're entirely English and you belong here, and that's the point. All you're going to do is tie yourself up in knots—mental, emotional—the lot.'

'I don't think so. At all events, I'm going, and that's that.'

'I just wish I knew why,' Peter said emphatically.

Brianna sighed. She was very fond of Peter, and they had

always got along well together. Their relationship was a warm one that hovered between the sisterly and brotherly and the lightly flirtatious. His parents, with whom she had spent this evening—her last in England for an unspecified period—wanted them to marry. Mrs Arden had exclaimed several times during dinner that she mustn't stay away too long, but come back before summer was over. They would miss her; Peter would miss her. In fact, she had all but put it in words that she wanted and expected her and Peter to marry as soon as he was through his teacher training course. She had got through all that safely, and now Peter had begun to heckle her about the whys and the wherefores of this journey she was about to make to Paris. At least he had the sense not to bring love and marriage into it. At his age, she didn't think he was any more ready than she was for marriage. The idea had appealed more to her grandmother and to his parents.

But it was too bad of Peter to try to unsettle her now, and she could only conclude that, with the possibility—a very slight one, if he only knew it—of her disappearing for ever and making her home permanently in France, he was beginning to feel possessive. She looked across at him ruefully. He was quite a handsome boy, with his curly brown hair and warm brown eyes, and he looked even younger than his twenty-one years and often acted it.

'You do know why I'm going,' she argued. 'Allowing myself to be a stranger to my own mother—my own sister—has been on my conscience for a long time. And now my mother's made the gesture and invited me to Paris, I have the opportunity I want, and I must take it, Peter, I really must, before it's too late. She's been ill in hospital, you know, and I might be some help while she's convalescing.' She sent him a pleading look. 'Can't you put yourself in my place? Imagine if *you* hadn't seen your mother for seven years, didn't even really know her—wouldn't you want——'

'Oh, don't expect me to do mental gymnastics, for heaven's sake,' he interrupted. 'The thing is, Bri, your mother doesn't deserve to have you anything but a stranger, seeing she deserted you when you were a mere child.'

'I was nine—and she didn't desert me, as you put it. You might just as well say my father deserted Isabelle. It was just a case of a marriage that didn't work, and when they separated they took one child each. That's not so hard to understand, is it? You or I might do the same thing too if we were in a similar situation. Who's to say? I was naturally the one who stayed in England because I was older and I'd started school. I'd have had a battle with the language in France, so it was fairer that way.'

Peter smiled slightly, his brown eyes mocking. 'Now come on, Bri, don't try to persuade me that everything in the garden's lovely, or ever was. I know better than that. I've heard stories from your grandmother. The French lot haven't given you a fair deal—dragging you to Paris the year your father died, and practically pulling you to pieces there. Your grandmother told my mother you couldn't get back home to her again fast enough, and she was months repairing the damage that had been done to your ego. Anglophobes, she said they were. Hated everyone and everything English.'

'Gran was inclined to exaggerate,' Brianna said uncomfortably. 'And if you must know, I behaved abominably the few weeks I spent in Paris.' She bit her lip. 'I feel so ashamed when I remember some of the things I did. It's been in my mind for some time that I should go back and put things right.'

Peter took out cigarettes and offered her one mechanically, and she shook her head, crossing her long slender legs and looking thoughtfully at her elegant green sandals. She knew quite well it was not going to be easy to put things right. In fact, it might prove to be quite impossible. She hadn't endeared herself to the French, and nor had they endeared themselves to her. She had been a schoolgirl, nearly fifteen, tallish and awkward, with no social aplomb, no dress sense, gauche and immature in every way. Illogically, under the circumstances, she had been angry with her mother for marrying again, and though she would not admit it even to Peter, she realised now that it was her grandmother who had been responsible for that anger. Gran, in fact, had never liked the French girl her only son had brought home to England as his bride, and when, less than six months after his death, Lucie had remarried, she had reviled her.

'To marry so soon after your father's death, Brianna! She has no feelings—she never did have any feelings except for what was across the Channel. This man, Jacques d'Hellier —she was probably having an affair with him all the time Malcolm was still alive. Quite likely she left your father for him and all this talk of living with her mother was a blind. No, I don't trust the French.'

In fact, she had never trusted the French, and she had never allowed Brianna to go back, her reason being her increasing ill health and need of her granddaughter. And because her first experience had been so unpleasant, Brianna hadn't really been tempted to try again, but now she did want to try, she regretted the past deeply ...

She said aloud, 'It's an awful feeling to be at war with your own flesh and blood. I just want to—to wipe it all out and begin again, so please, Peter, don't start filling my mind with unpleasant thoughts. This time I want to visit my French relatives—my stepfather and his family—with an open mind. With—with positive thoughts of friendliness.'

Peter looked across at her thoughtfully. 'All this wouldn't by any chance have something to do with that handsome French stepbrother of yours my mother told me about, who came to see you just after your grandmother died, would it?'

'Philippe?' To her great annoyance she coloured. 'No, of course not! Why should it have?'

'Well, you just might want to impress him——'

'Except I don't,' she said tersely. 'As far as I'm concerned, he's not all that handsome, and in any case he doesn't live in Paris, he lives in Burgundy on the Côte d'Or.'

'Really? Don't tell me he's a *vigneron*!'

'Yes, he is.'

'Romantic,' Peter commented. 'I don't wonder my mother was carrying on at you about coming back to us before too long. After meeting him, she can just picture you falling for all that French charm.'

'Well, it's the last thing that's likely to happen,' Brianna said. 'I'd never get myself involved with a Frenchman— not after the mess my parents made of their marriage. French and English just don't mix, in my experience.'

Peter grinned. 'If you really believe that, then you've just admitted that you're crazy!' He glanced at his watch and stood up. 'I'd better let you get to bed and brace yourself for the big adventure. And I'll be honest with you, Bri —I'll be weaving spells all the while you're away and hoping very meanly that French and English aren't mixing and that you'll be packing your bags and coming home for good.' He reached out a hand and pulled her to her feet. 'Miserable, aren't I? I'll grant you a few concessions—I hope you prove to your mother that you've grown up into a nice girl who knows how to behave, and you have my permission to impress your little sister favourably too, and henceforth to write her letters and send her gifts from England. But as far as the born and bred d'Helliers go— I hope you see all you ever want to see of them in the first twenty-four hours of your visit.' He stopped, grimaced, and admitted, 'I'm going to miss you.' Then before she could demur, he kissed her.

Brianna felt a slight sense of panic. Another minute, and he'd be telling her he loved her—and that *would* be the result of one of his mother's spells . . .

She said quickly, 'It's nice of you to say so, Pete. But there's never been any talk of my living with them permanently, you know. Maman is concerned that I'm on my own here, I suppose, but how long I stay depends how we get on together. It will have to be a little while, you can't expect to heal a breach like the one between us in a week or so. But you never know—they might kick *me* out,' she ended facetiously.

'I almost hope they do,' said Peter. 'But not quite,' he added. 'Well, goodnight. And write to me, won't you?'

'Of course,' she agreed cheerfully as she saw him to the door.

When he had gone, she tidied the sitting room, emptied the ashtray, and went thoughtfully upstairs to her room. The Martins' light was out and the house was quiet. Her room looked strangely bare, and the two suitcases on the floor, not yet locked, were a sharp reminder that tomorrow afternoon she would be leaving England. She got ready for bed, then lay in the dark, her mind too much stimulated to sleep for a long time.

Mrs Arden was quite wrong in her suspicions that Brianna might be attracted to Philippe. Quite definitely she wasn't. She supposed he was handsome—in a very French way—but somehow there was a deeply rooted hostility between them and even after seven years she was very much aware of it. The fact was, he had witnessed some of her very worst behaviour at the d'Hellier apartment, and she could never forget the contemptuous and pitying way he had looked at her, though he had made absolutely no comment on her conduct within her hearing. She had meant it when she had implied she didn't want to see much of him, because to be in his company, she had discovered quite recently, was a most disquieting experience and she had no wish to repeat it.

She had suffered far more than she could ever tell anyone all those years ago when she had gone to live in Paris with the family her mother had acquired when she remarried. The whole venture had been a disaster, and though Maman had cried over her before she went back to England, and though she herself had wept too—bitter, bitter tears, the meaning of which she hadn't understood—she had never wanted to go back. Never.

Those few weeks had been utter misery. She had felt a complete outsider. Language had been a big problem, the d'Helliers weren't interested in trying to communicate in English, and her schoolgirl French was hopeless. As well, she had been deeply conscious of being horribly different from the other members of the household. Her clothes were so uninterestingly sensible, she had no style. Even little Isabelle was more fashion-conscious than Brianna, whose wardrobe had for years been chosen by her grandmother. As for the d'Hellier girls, Honorine, seventeen, and Marie-Claude, a little younger than Brianna, they were very chic. Marie-Claude had made fun of her, in a way that hurt more because she couldn't properly understand what was being said. It was not at all agreeable to be patronised by a girl younger than herself but infinitely more assured. She had been utterly wretched and totally bewildered, and she had hated everyone and spent more time sulking alone in her room than was believable.

Maman hadn't known how to deal with the girls' hostility to each other, and besides, much of her time was taken up with Isabelle, a thin, headachey, somewhat neurotic little girl. On one occasion when Marie-Claude mocked her French accent, Brianna had hurled a book at her and

bruised her cheek, and Maman had called her a little
barbarian.

As well as the girls, there were two sons in the d'Hellier
family. Paul, the younger, was already working for his
father, who was a wine merchant and shipper with offices
in Paris and Dijon, and Philippe, except for those two days
that Brianna hated to remember, had been in Burgundy at
Huchet-les-Anges, learning from his maternal grandfather
the art of wine-making. As for Monsieur d'Hellier himself,
a big dark-haired, dark-eyed man some fourteen or fifteen
years older than Brianna's mother, she had mutinously refused to have anything to do with him.

She wondered now if she would have made more effort
to be agreeable if her grandmother hadn't assured her that
she would be wretchedly unhappy amongst the foreigners,
and that if she wanted she must come back home at once
—'to where you belong'.

'You're needed here, darling—you're all I have. You're
not needed or wanted there, but your mother's asked for
you, and I have to let you go even though I know very well
you won't fit in. The French are just not like us—you're in
for some shocks.'

Honorine and Paul were both married now, Philippe had
told Brianna. But Marie-Claude was not—Marie-Claude
who had reminded her often that it was *her* father's house
where Brianna was staying, and that everything in it belonged to her father. The fragile cup Brianna broke—'You
clumsy English!'—the Aubusson carpet on which she spilt
some coffee—the big square bed pillow that Brianna complained about—all belonged to Monsieur d'Hellier, and
Brianna was an uncultured *anglaise* who could not appreciate such refinements.

Perhaps Peter was right and she was crazy to be going
back to it—putting her head in the lion's jaws. If it had been
only Maman and Isabelle, it would have been all right. But

no, it was the whole family, and they were so close, all of them. Maman had even sent Philippe to Canterbury to see if Brianna needed any help after her grandmother had died. She hadn't come herself. But that could have been because she wasn't well.

He had arrived unannounced the day after the funeral, on an afternoon when she was alone in the house and aware of the fact that her life as from now would be very much changed. Her grandmother had been a semi-invalid for the past two years, and so Brianna had never had a full-time job. Not that she needed it. Her father had left her well provided for, and her grandmother had property that gave her a good income. She had worked part time in Peter's father's bookshop, which gave her a break from the house that was very welcome. She made time, too, to attend a French language class, something she had meant to do for a long time. She had studied French at school, but Marie-Claude's laughter at her efforts at expressing herself had brought it home to her painfully that schoolgirl French was not enough. Enough for what, she was not certain, and perhaps it was mainly a matter of pride that drove her on to master the language. She would not be caught out again, if ever circumstances brought her back into contact with her stepsister.

She had doubted that this would ever happen, for her only communication with the d'Helliers for a long time was a Christmas letter to her mother and sister, and a card to the family in general, and if sometimes she felt vaguely unhappy about this and once even expressed some of her feelings to Gran, she was told, 'Don't worry about them, darling. They're not worrying about you. They're content with each other, and you're content with me and with your English friends, aren't you?'

Yes, Brianna supposed she was content, and she tried to shelve her feelings of unease.

She wrote to her mother when Gran died, and in reply received a warm letter of condolence that somehow surprised her. It also contained an invitation to come to Paris now she was alone, and that she found surprising too—as if everything in the past had been forgiven and forgotten. Her immediate impulse was to go at once, but of course there were things to be done in connection with her grandmother's affairs before she could even think of going away, and if she were to go to France, it would be foolish to go for no more than a couple of days.

Perhaps she should talk it over with Mr Arden, she thought. But on the other hand, it was a very personal matter, and one that she would really have to decide for herself. Besides, she was not quite certain exactly what the invitation meant—whether her mother wanted her to live with the d'Helliers as part of the family, or whether she was merely making a friendly gesture. She was not really alone in the world—she had the Ardens, as well as a number of other friends, and she was quite able to support herself. The best thing to do, she decided, would be to write a warm sort of answer, saying she would love to come but that just now she had things to do that would keep her in England. After that—well, perhaps her mother's next communication would be a little more explicit. 'Come for a week, or a month, or indefinitely'—or whatever it was she had in mind.

She was actually in the midst of composing her letter when the doorbell rang, and answering it she was confronted by a man whom she recognised almost at once, and with a curious shock, as Philippe d'Hellier. He couldn't possibly be anyone else. He was so decidedly French...

For several seconds they simply looked at each other wordlessly, and she wondered what was going on in his mind. He must know who she was, as he had obviously come to see her, but she was aware that she was vastly changed from the wretched, rebellious and awkward schoolgirl she had been when last they met. What he saw now was a tallish, rather thin girl in jeans and plain blue shirt, her face completely bare of make-up, her straight light brown hair falling untidily across her cheeks. Nothing impressive, little sophistication—but surely an improvement.

As for him—he was totally mature, slim and broad-shouldered with excellent carriage. He had lean cheeks, a strong nose, and a mouth that was sensual in an ascetic, intelligent face, high-browed and Gallic, dominated by penetrating sapphire blue eyes.

With an effort she drew her glance away from those eyes, feeling the blood that had rushed to her cheeks recede to leave her pale. He moved too, lifting one eyebrow and saying with the trace of a cool smile, 'It *is* Brianna Gaze, isn't it?'

'Yes.' His voice surprised her, the accent scarcely discernible. 'You're Philippe d'Hellier, aren't you? I—I wasn't expecting you. Will you come inside?'

'Thank you.'

She led him nervously to the sitting room, aware that for some reason or other she needed to pull herself together. His presence had shaken her. As he took a chair at her invitation, she was conscious of the quick appraising look around the room. None of the elegant antiques that graced the d'Hellier apartment, but all the same, the furniture was good, and it had been well cared for. The pictures on the walls, though not originals, were excellent prints of Old Masters—her grandmother's taste. None of it, she was positive, was to *his* taste, but why should she care?

The next few minutes passed in a kind of haze. She hardly listened as he expressed regret at her grandmother's death and apologised that the d'Helliers had not been represented at the funeral. She found herself almost completely overwhelmed by a flood of painful memories that she had suppressed for a long time—memories of those last two or three days in Paris, when matters reached such a climax that the culmination was that she was sent back to England. She had been at her very worst then, with the dreaded prospect of the school year beginning, and she had run away —spent a whole long traumatic day on the Métro, and had Maman in a panic wondering what had happened to her. The police had been called in when she finally turned up, exhausted and weary-eyed, well after midnight.

Philippe, whom she had not met before, was there, one more unfriendly person in a world that seemed to her to be wholly hostile. She had refused to talk and she had refused to eat, and she had continued in this vein all through the following day. She remembered still the way Philippe had looked at her as she sat at the table, silent and white-faced, ignoring her food, ignoring everyone. She had thought, holding her head up defiantly, despite the fact that she was positively shrivelling up inside, that Philippe looked at her as if she were a creature so contemptible she was beyond his understanding. She didn't know what he had to say about her at the family conclave that was held that night, but the next morning after he left for the country, she was told she would not after all be going to school in Paris. She could finish her education in England. Her clothes and books were packed up and she was taken out to the airport that very day and put on the plane for London. And it was then that her mother had cried so bitterly.

She had not seen Philippe again since that day.

Now she dragged herself free of her unhappy recollections to hear him ask coolly, 'Your mother's letter reached you?'

'Today,' she nodded. 'I was—I was just trying to answer it.'

'Trying?' he repeated. 'Is it so difficult?'

'No, but you see, she's invited me to France——'

'I know that, and I'm aware it's probably not an idea that would appeal to you much. France isn't one of your favourite countries, is it? Are you trying to think how to say no?'

Brianna flushed deeply and moistened her lips, but didn't answer. His glance licked over her like a blue flame, and instinctively she shrank within herself, feeling a terrible stirring of doubt. Perhaps after all it would be too much of an ordeal to go back amongst the d'Helliers. She was ready to forget the past, to start again, but very possibly they were not. Certainly she hadn't endeared herself to them up till now, and they might well prefer to live without her.

Philippe narrowed his brilliantly blue eyes and continued, 'Frankly, if you're unwilling, I can see very little point in your coming. It's too late in so many ways, now you're no longer a child. However, your mother was anxious to make the gesture at this particular time, and I thought it wise to find out at any rate if you're in any sort of need—if there's anything we can do for you.'

He paused and this time she did speak, resenting his coldly aloof tone.

'No, I'm not in any sort of need. There's nothing at all any of you can do for me. I need neither pity nor help, Philippe. My father provided for me, and I'm my grandmother's sole beneficiary. Also, though you may find it hard to believe, I do have friends in England—quite a few of them. Affectionate friends,' she concluded haughtily, and looked at him very directly.

'I'm glad of that,' he said levelly. 'Nevertheless, out of politeness and consideration for your mother's feelings, I think you should visit her since she wishes it, even if you spend no more than two or three days in France.'

'Do you really?' Brianna felt jolted by his perfunctory manner. 'Well, it doesn't really matter a great deal to me what you think, and I certainly don't need you to teach me what's polite or right. I'd already decided to accept my mother's invitation. My problem is fixing on a date when I can go.'

'I see.' He didn't look as if he believed her, and his glance was sceptical. 'Then I think I can settle that for you—'

'No, thank you. I'm quite capable of deciding for myself,' she flashed. 'As it happens I have a number of things to see to before I'm free, and it all depends when they get sorted out. That's what I was trying to explain in my letter.'

'Then we can reach a point of agreement,' he said with a shrug. 'As it happens, a visit would be inadvisable just now. Your mother is being admitted to hospital for a minor operation very shortly—there's nothing to worry about, we've been assured, so don't make a melodrama of it and think you have to pack your bags and take the plane the minute I leave the house ... The best thing for you to do will be to wait until she's home again and recovered, since there's no emergency at this end, before you think of——' He paused, and the words 'inflicting yourself on us' slipped into Brianna's mind, but he didn't say them. Instead he finished with an ironic smile, 'Before you honour us with your presence.'

'Very well,' she said stiffly. 'I'll wait.' She would have liked to say she was sorry her mother had to go into hospital, but she found she couldn't. Anyhow, he would probably think it insincere.

'I'll keep in touch with you, Brianna,' he said after a moment. 'I hope you'll trust me to know best when your mother will be able to see you.'

To see her! It sounded, she thought wryly, as if she were to do no more than—pop across the Channel for afternoon tea, as it were. Certainly her mother's invitation was indefinite, but equally certainly it had more substance to it than that.

'Thank you,' she said with reluctant politeness, aware of

a slight sense of relief that she didn't have to face 'them' yet. She added after a brief pause, 'How is Isabelle?'

'Your sister's well. Still at school, but growing up fast. She's sixteen now, and very, very pretty.'

'Oh.' Somehow she was surprised at this description of Isabelle. At nine or so, she had been small and thin, always complaining of headaches, and with dark circles under her eyes. 'And the—others?' she added with an effort.

It was then he told her that Honorine and Paul were married. 'Paul has two children, as perhaps you know.'

No, she hadn't known. Her mother had never written her newsy letters.

'And—you, Philippe?' she asked, though she hadn't meant to. 'You're not married yet?'

'Not yet,' he agreed uncommunicatively, and it was at this point that Peter's mother, who had come into the house through the back door, appeared in the sitting room, and paused, evidently taken aback to find Brianna with a strange man.

Philippe got to his feet and Brianna made the introductions.

'So you're Brianna's stepbrother from France! Well, what a surprise!' Mrs Arden exclaimed. 'How lovely to meet you. I've heard so much——' She paused and glanced at Brianna. 'Are you going to make some tea, dear, or would you like me to do that for you?'

'No, I'll see to it, of course,' Brianna said hurriedly, and disappeared promptly to the kitchen to put the kettle on. She felt annoyed with herself for not having thought to offer Philippe some refreshment, and wondered if he might prefer coffee. The d'Helliers, she recalled, had drunk coffee constantly. 'Well, he's in England now,' she decided, 'and we have tea in the afternoon, so he can like it or lump it!'

She felt slightly anxious leaving him with Mrs Arden, who was a bit of a character and so adept at the art of filling silences she was inclined to be a bore. She would probably drone on and on about the garden and Peter and her trip to London and heaven knew what else, but for sure there would be not one second of silence. Brianna decided to leave her to it and was tempted to run upstairs and change out of her jeans into something a little more impressive—to apply some make-up, and tidy her hair. But she refrained. She had already seen Philippe's opinion of her in those sapphire blue eyes of his, and she didn't think a change of clothing was likely to alter it.

When she carried in the tea tray, Mrs Arden was talking about Gran—and of what a great joy to her Brianna had been. He wouldn't believe she could be a joy to anyone, Brianna reflected, as she broke in gently to ask if he took milk or lemon.

She had no further conversation alone with him after that. Mrs Arden spent some time busily emphasising that in the Arden family, Brianna had close and loving friends who would see her safely through any crisis.

'You set my mind very much at rest, *madame*,' Philippe managed to put in at last. 'In France we were wondering if Brianna would now need the support of the d'Hellier family. Instead, it appears her life is full and happy and that she has no need of her French relatives.'

'No indeed!' Mrs Arden gave a light laugh. 'Brianna has all the friends she needs here in England. Our home is hers any time she needs it.'

Philippe turned to Brianna. 'This isn't your house? You have to leave it?'

'Oh dear me, no.' Mrs Arden spoke for her. 'This is Brianna's house. Her father willed it to her when he died, and it will be a lovely home for her when she marries. Meanwhile, rather than live here on her own, which wouldn't be very pleasant, my husband advised her to find a nice young married couple and share it with them until everything's sorted out.'

'That sounds like a good plan,' Philippe nodded, and again addressed Brianna. 'I begin to wonder if you'll be able to find time to visit your mother at all.'

'Of course I shall,' Brianna said crossly. 'If you or my mother will let me know when it's convenient, I'll certainly come. My mother wants me to visit her,' she explained to Mrs Arden, who was looking puzzled and curious.

'Really, dear? That would be nice if you could manage it. There's such a lot to see in Paris, and now you're old enough to appreciate it you'd really enjoy yourself. Charles and I had a week there before Peter was born—we have such lovely memories.' She paused and before she could continue Philippe was on his feet.

'Please excuse me, *madame*, but it's time for me to go. It's been a pleasure to meet you and to know that my step-sister has such good friends.' He turned to Brianna, who rose and saw him to the door. She was surprised that he had stayed so short a time, but she was relieved too, and she didn't dare ask him where he was going or even if he was staying in England. At the door, he repeated that he would be in touch with her, then bowed slightly and strode off, and she went inside feeling utterly frustrated without really knowing why.

'He's off to London, I suppose,' Mrs Arden said when she rejoined her in the sitting room.

'I don't really know,' Brianna admitted. 'He didn't say. Should I—do you think I should have asked him to stay?'

'What? Overnight? Alone in the house with you—or as good as? My dear, I should say not! It wouldn't be proper.'

'But the Martins are here—and he's my stepbrother,' Brianna said slowly. That feeling of frustration, she was beginning to think, had something to do with the fact that she hadn't had a chance to mention the past. She had been too upset at first. She would have liked an opportunity to—well, not exactly explain her frightful behaviour in Paris, and not exactly apologise for it either, but—oh, she didn't know what she'd wanted to do. She did know that something needed to be said to bring about an understanding of some sort, though his manner wasn't what you would call encouraging, and quite likely she would never have got around to saying anything at all.

Meanwhile, Mrs Arden had given a brief snort of laughter. 'Your stepbrother!' she exclaimed. 'I can imagine what the neighbours would think if a striking man like that stayed with you overnight! Now that he's gone, I think you can forget him, Brianna. I know all about your French relatives from your grandmother, and I haven't much time for them. He's merely done his duty in coming to see you—the family honour is no doubt satisfied. As for your mother's invitation to visit her in Paris, I'd take that with a grain of salt. It's no more than a gesture. You certainly don't owe it to her to go. She's hardly been a good mother to you, and it would merely stir up some old unhappy memories. It's for you to decide, of course, dear, but my advice is to suit yourself and not allow sentiment to blind you.'

Several weeks passed after that before Brianna heard from France again. Then, there was no word from her mother but a letter from Philippe explaining that Maman had been kept in hospital longer than expected, and suggesting a date for a visit—a date which she had at once confirmed.

And now that day had come at last.

No one was at the airport at Orly to meet her when her plane landed lateish in the afternoon. Somehow, she had expected Philippe. In fact, she had braced herself for the meeting, studied her reflection in her hand-mirror before the plane landed, put a little more shade on her eyelids, attended to the curve of her rather wide mouth, hoped desperately—and rather idiotically—that she looked not so much British as international. Ridiculous, that, when she was very, very, insular and quite aware of it. She hadn't ventured outside the United Kingdom since before her fifteenth birthday.

Now, as there was no one to meet her, she must manage for herself. Thank heaven for the French lessons, she thought, having emerged successfully from Customs and looked about her in vain for a familiar face. She finally rejected the idea of taking a bus in to Invalides, and instead got herself a taxi. Possibly she would be overcharged, she reflected nervously, as the taxi sped along the Autoroute du Sud in the direction of Paris, but she didn't come to France every day of the week and she was not exactly penniless. Her nervousness was increasing, and her attempts to distract herself by trying to recognise landmarks were quite futile. As a schoolgirl, she had been too wrapped up in her own misery to be interested in Paris—oh God! the opportunities she had missed!—and she knew very well that nothing short of the Eiffel Tower was likely to arouse memories or to look familiar in any way.

All the same, she was aware of a vague stirring when at last they reached the quarter where the d'Helliers lived. Yes—this street, the supermarket, the *pâtisserie*, the little bistro—she remembered them with a pain that had little pleasure in it, but a strong aura of some kind of regret. And there was the Métro station from which she had started her mad day of disappearance—

It was late evening and though it was August, a month when half the population of Paris deserted the city for holidays elsewhere, the streets were crowded with people. She remembered with a sickening vividness the sound of incomprehensible French voices, and her own bitter conviction that everyone in this country hated her. But of course they hadn't!—of course they hadn't! She remembered too her mother's tears when they had parted. How she had wept! Perhaps her tears had been shed not only because her daughter had rejected her, but because in taking on the responsibility of a step-family, she had burdened herself with more problems than she had expected. Such thoughts hadn't entered Brianna's head seven years ago, she had thought only of herself, and in the plane she had cried too. In fact, she had wept so much that she had been a complete wreck when her grandmother met her at Heathrow ...

Now as she got out of the taxi and paid the driver, she felt as if she were suffering an attack of stage fright. It was one thing to make up your mind you were going to make friends with your family, and quite another thing to do it, especially when you were so very much ashamed of the girl you had been. But at least this time she was armed with a knowledge of the French language—though even that weapon, she presently discovered, was blunted, because her mother very determinedly spoke English to her.

The d'Helliers lived on the sixteenth floor of the apartment block, and once Brianna had satisfied the concierge as to her identity, she was carried swiftly upwards in the elevator. She found herself remembering how one could look through the big windows of the salon away out towards the trees that grew by the Seine, and at night were floodlit so that they looked an unearthly and beautiful green. And all around lights floated on the dark sea of the summer night, and there was a humming and a vibration in the air as if the great heart of Paris were beating. Brianna stepped out of the *ascenseur* blinking slightly, surprised by her own thoughts. Had she noticed such things at fourteen? Or had she looked without seeing, and only now, as she returned, was she interpreting—*feeling*—what she had seen and heard?

Someone she didn't know let her into the apartment. She was keyed up to expect Isabelle or Marie-Claude, but it was a strange girl who she realised was the maid. And then her stepfather came to greet her—swarthy-faced, brown-eyed, murmuring *'Enchanté*!' over her hand, and asking her questions in French that she knew concerned her journey but that she couldn't answer because suddenly she was quite terrified. She felt herself too tangibly carried back into the past, so that instead of being a smartly dressed, reasonably poised young woman, she seemed to be still the gauche, ungracious schoolgirl of long ago—a nuisance, a nightmare, a problem to everyone.

But *he* seemed unaware of that, and presently having relinquished her luggage to the maid, Henriette, Brianna was in the salon and her mother was welcoming her with the customary kiss on either cheek.

'Brianna! But how charming you are looking! Please sit down. You would like some tea? Jacques——' She had been speaking English, but now she switched to French, and Jacques summoned Henriette to order tea, then disappeared himself, leaving the two women alone.

Brianna sat down and looked at her mother a little warily. She was small and vivacious, her hair still dark, but after all, she was still in her early forties. Her face was too thin, and her eyes darkly shadowed, and behind her animated manner was a decided hint of nervousness and strain. She looked, in fact, very fragile, and Brianna recalled Philippe said she had been kept in hospital longer than expected.

'You 'ave 'ad a good journey, Brianna?'

'Yes, very pleasant, thank you, Maman.' Brianna had the awful feeling she was speaking to a stranger. But what had she imagined? Tears? Kisses? A warm embrace? No, not really. But perhaps *some* sort of sign that the past was over and forgotten, that they could now reach an understanding. And she was taken by surprise to find that English was being spoken, which deprived her of the opportunity of airing her knowledge of French. She began to realise it wasn't going to be easy to acquire a real mother. It might be less of a problem to get on to close terms with Isabelle, and that thought prompted her to ask, 'Is Isabelle here, Maman? And the—the others?'

'No, *ma chère*. Isabelle is in the country. Also Marie-Claude. You know perhaps that Honorine now lives in Nice? And Paul and Micheline 'ave gone to Venice.'

Brianna wanted to ask about Philippe, but didn't. Henriette brought in the tea, but Jacques didn't reappear, and Brianna reflected uneasily that no one was sufficiently interested to be here to greet her. She watched the stranger who was her mother lift the elegant white and gold teapot and pour tea into cups so small they looked like part of a doll's tea service. She was offered milk, sugar, a dish of fresh pastries.

The tea was appalling and barely hot, and Brianna couldn't help thinking the French had no idea how to serve it. As she sipped it, she had the curious feeling that she was quite definitely not going to be expected to stay here more than two or three days at the most. It was a gesture her mother had made, that was all.

'Ah yes,' her mother said after a minute. 'Everyone is away. It is August, you understand, and we are about to close up the apartment. Tomorrow Jacques takes me to Switzerland to convalesce. It is unfortunate, and I hope you will forgive me, Brianna. We have no more than greeted each other, but Philippe said you were anxious to come and I am happy you felt that way.' She smiled, but Brianna could hardly believe her ears. Tomorrow her mother was leaving for Switzerland! What a welcome to a daughter who had hoped to make amends for the past! She felt her heart freeze with anger against Philippe, who surely must have arranged this deliberately. He had never approved of her coming—he had said it was too late anyhow.

'I understand,' she heard herself saying calmly. 'If I'd known you were going away, I could have come sooner. I'm sorry you aren't well yet.'

'Please do not be concerned for me. It is nothing. Tonight Philippe will arrive. You must discuss with him what you would like to do. He will look after you ... Another cup of tea, *chèrie*?'

Brianna shook her head, feeling both miserable and angry. How right Peter had been! She was mad to have come. No one, not even her mother, really wanted her here. She was nothing more than a guest who had arrived at an inconvenient moment. As for allowing Philippe to look after her—she had parted her lips to say no, thank you to that, when she hesitated. Her mother did look ill, and instead she exclaimed brightly, 'I'm sure he'll look after me, Maman. You mustn't worry. We'll work it out between us. Please don't give it another thought—you must think only of getting your health back. You should be resting now, I'm sure. Shall I take the tray out to the kitchen?'

'No, no, Henriette will see to that. But perhaps if you will excuse me, I shall go to my room. I am tired, and tomorrow we must travel. I am happy to have been able to greet you and to know you are content to be left in Philippe's care. Perhaps we can hope to see a little more of each other before the year is out.'

'I hope so,' Brianna agreed.

It was not until after her mother had left the room that she really thought of what she had said about Philippe looking after her. She thought she could guess what that would mean. She had granted her mother's wish to see her, and now she could go home. He wouldn't hesitate to tell her so. But he was not going to have it all his own way, he was not going to force his will on her. Definitely not. Because she was going to insist on seeing Isabelle before she went, even though she was very much afraid that 'in the country' meant in Huchet-les-Anges, where Philippe had his vineyards. The idea of practically inviting herself there was a far from palatable one, but Philippe would just have to put up with her. Which was all very well in theory, but she wasn't really confident she would be able to persuade him to have her there.

She didn't wait up that night to see Philippe when he arrived. Her mother went to bed very early, and rather than sit with her stepfather in the salon, she pleaded tiredness and went to her room. It wasn't the room she had slept in last time she was here. This room had been Honorine's and it held no memories. The carpet was soft and thick, and the windows looked down on to the enclosed square that was private to this apartment block. It was lighted by lamps and Brianna parted the curtains and looked down at the ordered paths and flower beds, strangely unreal and stylised from the sixteenth floor. A few people walked there, and high above, stars floated glimmeringly in the dark of the sky.

'Paris,' she thought wryly. 'Romantic Paris.' And all her hopes of starting anew were as far off as those distant stars. Tomorrow when she woke Philippe would be there ...

He was there, making a breakfast of coffee and croissants in the dining room where she had joined him. She wasn't hungry—she was too nervous for that—but she sat down at the table, nibbled at a croissant, drank some of the hot milky coffee, half expecting him to make some caustic comment on the fact that she was not on a hunger strike this time, because she was sure he remembered that as clearly as she did.

'So you came,' he said. 'I wondered if you would. It's unfortunate that Maman is leaving today.'

'Is it?' She looked at him sceptically over her coffee cup.

'But you knew, didn't you? You were the one who arranged when I was to come.'

'That was a week ago,' he said coldly. 'Events have changed. Your mother hasn't a strong constitution. Her recovery needs time. It wasn't I who said she must go to Switzerland, you know, the specialist ordered it. The fact is, she's not yet in a condition to cope with family problems.'

Family problems! 'Me,' thought Brianna, uncertain as to how much of what he said was true. He didn't bring up the subject of what was to be done with her, and neither did she. After breakfast, Philippe helped his parents complete their preparations for departure and Brianna was left to her own devices. She felt very much *de trop*. For her, the rest of the morning was a confusion of French voices, of comings and goings through the apartment, and then at last her mother had said goodbye.

'I leave you in Philippe's hands, *chérie*.'

Quite suddenly, she was alone in the apartment with her stepbrother.

CHAPTER TWO

BRIANNA disappeared to her room to finish her packing. Not that she had bothered unpacking many of her things, under the circumstances. She didn't imagine it would be possible for her to stay here, for Henriette, who had been hard at work cleaning and tidying all morning, had now departed, and already the apartment looked as if it weren't lived in. The curtains were drawn and the rooms looked strangely empty.

It was time to do some thinking, and Brianna wished she had done it last night instead of getting into a flap and alternately fuming and fretting over the predicament she was in. She had little doubt that as soon as he got her alone Philippe would tell her she must go back to England.

'But why should I?' she asked herself mutinously, standing by the window and looking out at the brightness of the summer day. She had gone to considerable trouble to come over to France with the intention of reopening communications with her family. She had gone to some expense too, come to that, because she had bought herself a heap of new clothes. And even though her mother had gone away, there was still Isabelle. So—damn Philippe d'Hellier! She would see her sister even if she had to invite herself to Huchet-les-Anges. Philippe surely wouldn't be so rude as to refuse to let her come.

But wouldn't he? She heard herself laugh mirthlessly. She was really fooling herself if she tried to believe that. He had a very low opinion of Brianna Gaze, the trouble-maker.

She started as he rapped sharply on the door.

'Are you there, Brianna?'

'Yes, I'm here. Where else would I be?' she answered half beneath her breath, but he had opened the door and heard her.

'I thought you might have run away for a ride on the Métro,' he said with a sardonic look. Then before she could gather her outraged senses to protest at that unfair reference to a past she preferred to forget, he continued, 'We'll go out and have some lunch—there's a little restaurant round the corner. How long do you need to be ready?'

'Five minutes,' she said briefly, and when he had nodded and moved away, she wondered why she had—sprung to attention so smartly, as it were. Well, perhaps it was the best thing to have done, seeing she wanted to ask a favour of him.

She changed quickly out of the pants and shirt she had worn to breakfast, then stood in the middle of the room and looked at herself critically in the mirror, liking the look of the simple green dress that emphasised the slenderness of her figure. Pale biscuit-coloured shoes and handbag completed her outfit, and the eye-shadow she wore blended well with the colour of her dress and brought out the gold in her eyes. Her eyebrows were straight and darker than her hair, and gave strength to a face that was otherwise very feminine —and very English, she reminded herself, half humorously. There was nothing of the provocative and mysterious Frenchwoman about Brianna Gaze!

It was more than ten minutes when she emerged from her room and finding Philippe in the salon, standing at the window with his back to the light, she said politely, 'I'm afraid I've taken longer than I said I would.'

'Please don't apologise. I expected it—not of you specifically,' he added with a frown at her instant look of indignation. 'Of any woman who's interested in her appearance.' His eyes took her in from head to toe, but he made no comment, though she had expected he might pay her a passing compliment. But after all, what had she ever done to deserve compliments?

'Come along, then,' he said, and she went ahead of him out of the apartment. Neither of them spoke as the lift carried them silently to the ground floor. He didn't take her arm or even touch it as they walked through the sunshine to the restaurant—one that she remembered vaguely seeing when she was here before, though she had never eaten there. It was an unpretentious little place, and they were soon seated opposite each other at a white-clothed table. Philippe ordered some kind of fish, a salad, and a carafe of white wine.

'That will do, I think,' he remarked when the waiter had departed. 'It will be no more than a meal, but then we're not celebrating anything, are we?'

She felt a little chill and thought unreasonably, 'We *could* have been celebrating my return to France.'

The carafe of wine was brought and he poured a little into each of their glasses, broke the crust from one of the rolls in the basket on the table and looked at her with disconcerting directness. Somehow his handsome French arrogance set her nerves trembling and made her weak at the knees so that she was glad she was sitting down. She had the sudden feeling that she couldn't possibly win if there was conflict between them over what was to be done with her. She could picture herself doing exactly as he said— and hating herself for it afterwards. She reached for her glass and drank down some of the wine as if hoping it would give her strength and conviction.

'So now we are alone,' he said then. 'And it's been left to me to plan your movements.'

'Has it?' Brianna raised her clear hazel eyes to his with a touch of defiance. 'I understood you were to—look after me.'

'That's one way of putting it,' he agreed. 'But I have my own ideas as to what should be done, and what you may happen to want to do doesn't come at the top of my list.'

'But what *you* want me to do does?'

'Of course.' The waiter appeared with their order and when they were alone again, he pushed the salt and pepper towards her, picked up his knife and fork, and resumed the conversation.

'I'm quite aware you've been brought up to dislike my country and my countrymen, and I suppose you're satisfied you've done your duty in coming to Paris for this fleeting visit——'

'How dare you suppose any such thing?' she interrupted indignantly. 'You—you tricked me—you arranged it all. It's not my fault I've had no more than time to say hello and goodbye to my mother, so why on earth should I feel satisfied with that, having come all this way?'

'Now calm down and don't be so ready to blame me,' he said reasonably. 'I've already explained what happened, and I'll add now that your mother, knowing how—sensitive you are, didn't want to hurt your feelings by putting you off. So now it's your turn to do the considerate thing—the right thing—which is what I want you to do.'

'Yes?' she said, bristling at his attitude. 'And what *is* the right thing, in your opinion?' She took a mouthful of fish without tasting it, her cheeks flushed.

'You'll come with me to Huchet-les-Anges and make an effort to be pleasant to your mother's family for a change. Tante Agathe is there—your sister, Marie-Claude, and Paul and Micheline's two infants. And myself, of course.'

'What?' She stared at him almost stupidly. To think he wanted her to do exactly what she had planned to do! She could have laughed except that she felt furious with herself for letting him get in first with it—and imagine that he was teaching her manners!

'Don't I make myself clear?'

'Perfectly clear,' she said coldly. 'But I dislike intensely being told what I must do, as if I were completely lacking in reason.'

He shrugged. 'It's possible to persuade oneself that one's acting reasonably on almost any occasion. I simply want to make sure you forget any ideas you might have about running away back to England and your Englishman and conveniently forgetting the existence of the d'Helliers once more.'

'I'm sure I shall never forget *you*,' she said with an icy smile. 'But let me assure you it's not only the French who know the right thing to do, and for your information I had no intention of running back to England and my Englishman, whatever you mean by that.'

'Oh, come along now—you forget you left me alone with your fiancé's mother while you made tea that day in Canterbury! I know you have reasons for wanting to go back home again.'

Brianna sighed inwardly. Had Mrs Arden actually told him that she and Peter were engaged? she wondered with a feeling of exasperation. Yet it didn't matter much one way or the other, and she brushed aside his remarks impatiently.

'Well, whatever you know or think you know, I don't have it in mind to go back to England yet. I want to see my sister, and I'll welcome the opportunity of proving to at least *some* members of the d'Hellier family that though I'm English and——' She paused, then forced herself to go on. 'And though I behaved badly when I was fourteen, I'm not really a monster. I can see you don't want to be convinced, so I shan't put myself out to impress you. It's just a pity you happen to be part of the family, because I think I'm going to find it rather hard to like you.'

They stared at each other across the table, and Brianna refused to blink or to look away. Then his lips twisted wryly and he remarked indifferently, 'Unfortunately the feeling's mutual.'

They finished their meal in silence, though Brianna ate scarcely another mouthful. She hoped desperately that Tante Agathe, whom she had not met, would not prove to be hard to get on with, or prejudiced against her because of what had happened years ago; that Marie-Claude would be reasonably pleasant. Because, come to think of it, Marie-Claude had been decidedly disagreeable herself. No one could have called *her* welcoming to the stepsister from England. One part of her would have given anything in the world to have got up from the table and walked away right now, so as never to see Philippe d'Hellier and his family again. But on the other hand, her whole reason for coming to France was to undo the mistakes of the past—and perhaps, incidentally, to discover if she disliked the French as much as her grandmother had done.

So she was simply not going to let her stepbrother's high-handedness frighten her away. The best thing to do would be to pretend to herself that this conversation had never happened. She would go with him to Huchet-les-Anges and carry out her own plans, and ignore him as far as it was possible.

'Shall we go?' Philippe asked into her thoughts, and without answering she rose from the table obediently and moved towards the door.

She enjoyed the long drive to Huchet-les-Anges despite the constraint between herself and Philippe. She had no previous experience of the French countryside, and the vastness and openness of it surprised her, as did the very rural nature of many of the small towns and villages they passed through. The wine-growing country of Burgundy she found completely charming. She had never seen vines growing and they were so leafy and luxurious-looking—

acres and acres of them, spreading across the broad valleys and up the slopes of hills that were crowned with cool dark forests. She would have liked to ask a million questions, but she was still stinging from the conversation she had had with Philippe. Her feelings were hurt, she felt prejudged and disliked, and she kept silent, merely feasting her eyes on the green growing things of summer.

Finally they turned off the Route Nationale on to a smaller country road where a sign pointed to Armette.

'Armette is our nearest town,' Philippe explained easily, as if he had been unperturbed by her silence. 'Tante Agathe does much of her shopping there. Which reminds me—— But are you listening or do you prefer to ignore me, *belle-soeur*?'

'I'm listening,' she said, hating, for some reason, to have him call her stepsister, and feeling her fair cheeks flush with warm colour.

'Well then, I was about to say—to give you something to do with yourself while you're in Huchet—it might be a good idea if you and Isabelle got together and taught each other something of your own particular language. Isabelle learns English at school, but she's lazy and doesn't work at it, and as for you—you'll certainly find life in France easier if you try to understand the language. I recall you were hopelessly at sea there the last time you were in France. Was French one of your subjects at school?'

'Yes,' she said stiffly. She didn't feel ready to tell him she had worked hard at the language in the last couple of years and was now reasonably fluent. He could find that out for himself.

'Well, that's a start. I hope you haven't forgotten it all since you left.'

'No,' she said this time. It seemed odd that he preferred to speak to her in English instead of testing her out with French, but she supposed it was either politeness or patronage. It wouldn't occur to him that she might understand him quite well.

'You might also find time to help Tante Agathe with the infants,' he said presently. 'She's getting on in years, and Micheline would never have left them with her if she hadn't been sure there would be someone else to give a hand.'

'Isabelle and Marie-Claude are there, aren't they? She could hardly have been counting on me,' Brianna said, and realised too late how horribly ungracious she sounded. Actually she liked children, and had several times looked after Peter Arden's small niece. As well, the idea of having something useful to do was a relief, and she nearly added, 'Of course I'll help,' but she checked herself. She wasn't going to cringe, and she'd already said she wouldn't try to impress Philippe. He could take her as she was or leave her...

Once through Armette, they were in the country again, this time following a narrow road that wound its way through low rolling hills. As well as vineyards, there were ploughed fields and pastures and the occasional brilliance of red poppies by the roadside. Then, as they took a wide curve, an open valley stretched out ahead of them, and at its far end, tucked in among the vineyards, the grey roofs and houses and the slender spire of a village church were to be seen.

'That's Huchet,' Philippe remarked, a decided note of affection in his voice, as they drove quickly down the long winding slope into the valley.

'Huchet-les-Anges,' Brianna murmured. She knew that *les Anges* meant angels. 'Why is it called that, Philippe?'

'The name's taken from the largest vineyard in the area —the Clos des Anges.'

'Yours?' she asked.

'No, not mine. Clos des Anges was parcelled out long years ago, and now has many owners. Les Fleurons is my

property, and it's very much smaller, but well situated on
the slopes—a picked position for wine grapes.'

Brianna thought, as they took the level road across the
valley, and the golden light from the setting sun made a
haze on the hills and gilded the green of the vineyards, that
it was one of the prettiest and most romantic places she had
seen. On the outskirts of the village they passed a big old
house—a manor house, with vineyards stretching out behind it, very imposing-looking, and giving the impression
that it had been there for centuries.

'Is that the Clos des Anges?' she asked, looking back at it.

'No, that's Madame Hubert-Benoise's property,' he said
briefly, and added nothing to that.

The village was small, the streets narrow, once they had
left the village square with its garage, its *auberge*, its small
shops and its outdoor tables. There were stone walls and
iron gates, and beyond them Brianna glimpsed sometimes
a large old house, sometimes a simple one. At the far end
of the village, Philippe drove in through great grilled gates
and pulled up in a flagged courtyard, sheltered from the
street by a high wall on one side and low stone garages on
the other. Brianna felt a vague sense of disappointment.
She had expected his home would be set in the midst of
vineyards like the manor house they had passed earlier.
It was an imposing house none the less, two-storied with a
roof of glazed tiles patterned in typical Burgundian style.
The stone walls were warm-coloured, the shutters on the
windows blue-grey. A balustrade separated the courtyard
from a grassed terrace where there were flower beds bright
with roses and petunias and geraniums, and outdoor furniture was set out hospitably in the shade. Above, the great
leafy branches of chestnut trees spread against a sky now
flowered with the small apricot-coloured clouds of evening.

It all looked very welcoming, but no one came out to
meet them, and Brianna, standing by the car while Philippe

extracted the luggage, asked nervously, 'Are we—am I—expected?'

He sent her a sardonic look. 'Yes, you're expected. I had every intention of bringing you back with me. I don't make a practice of springing instant guests on Tante Agathe. She's kept house for me for a long time, and for my grandfather before me, and she's worthy of more consideration.' He nodded in the direction of the house. 'Go ahead, will you? Forget the baggage,' he added as she made a move to pick up one of the suitcases. 'I'll see to that.'

With a slight shrug she did as she was told.

Philippe pushed open a door by which grew a trellised vine with tiny green grapes on it and they went into a big square hallway from which several rooms opened.

'Tante Agathe is possibly attending to the children,' Philippe remarked, and the next second a prettily high-pitched voice called excitedly, 'C'est toi, Philippe?' and a young girl emerged from one of the rooms.

Brianna stared at her speechlessly, aware only an instant before Philippe told her so that this was Isabelle. In other circumstances, she would never have recognised her little sister in this vivacious young beauty—petite, with a peach-bloom complexion, black dancing eyes, and two short saucy corn-coloured pigtails whose ribbonned ends brushed provocatively against brown shoulders, revealed by the wide neck of a pale blue dress.

' 'Ello, Brianna!' Brianna received a quick brush of the lips on either cheek, but Isabelle evidently had other things on her mind besides the arrival of her English sister, for she whirled round instantly to tell Philippe, in French, 'I'm concocting an aperitif, Philippe. Violette gave me the recipe —two hundred peach leaves, loaf sugar—some red wine. Tomorrow I must add *eau de vie*, and *voilà*! a superb aperitif for you. You must come into the kitchen and see.'

'Oh, forget your aperitif,' he said impatiently, and

Brianna thought it rather offhand of him when the child
was so eager with her information. 'Take Brianna upstairs
to the room that's been prepared for her. And you'd better
start now practising your English,' he added, switching to
that language himself. 'Where's Marie-Claude?'

'She is gone to visit Louis. And Tante Agathe—she has
taken the infants for a walk. But I wished to be here when
you came.' She turned to Brianna '*Viens!* I take you to the
chambre d'amis.' She sent Philippe a coquettish smile, then
with a toss of her pigtails, she bounded up the stairs.
Brianna followed more sedately, but feeling considerably
cheered.

She caught up with Isabelle on a wide landing that was
furnished with a couple of comfortable-looking chairs, a
small chaise-longue, and a table on which were some books.
Isabelle indicated the latter and told Brianna in French,
'Marie-Claude's been working at her English. Do you understand what I'm saying?'

'Perfectly,' Brianna answered in the same language. It
seemed a good sign that Marie-Claude was brushing up her
English, and she hoped it was in her honour. If so, it
seemed possible that Marie-Claude too might want to make
amends for what had happened in the past.

'So you do speak French,' Isabelle remarked, whisking
off again up another short flight of stairs with Brianna following closely behind. 'Philippe said you didn't.'

'Well, I do—though not terribly well,' Brianna assured
her. Isabelle pushed open a door and stood aside for her to
enter. The *chambre d'amis*—the guest room. It was a
smallish room decorated almost entirely in blue—a soft blue
with a hint of grey in it. Blue curtains and bedspread, blue
and ivory carpet on the polished wood floor. The ceiling,
black-beamed, was a paler blue and the walls were white
plaster. The window looked over the narrow street by
which they had come through the village. Isabelle collapsed

on the low bed, equipped, Brianna noticed, with one of those huge square pillows that she had found so foreign and so unacceptable on her previous visit to France. Well, it wouldn't worry her now. In fact, anything that was different she would find interesting. She wandered across to the window and looked out. Beyond the houses across the street the hills rose, vine-covered and green in the declining light.

'France is not in the least like England,' she said aloud. 'Do you remember England at all, Isabelle?'

'No, not at all.'

'Would you like to go back?'

'Why should I? This is my country.'

'Yes. It's strange, isn't it?' Brianna left the window and sat on the end of the bed. 'You're French and I'm English, yet we're sisters.'

'I haven't got used to that yet,' said Isabelle. 'Do you mean to stay here long, Brianna?'

Brianna had no idea how to answer that, for her plans depended on a number of things. 'I'd like to stay here till Maman comes back from Switzerland,' she said cautiously. 'I only saw her for a short time last night, and this morning everyone was so busy we had no time to talk. I had no idea she'd been so ill.'

'I don't suppose it really matters to you,' Isabelle said candidly. 'You aren't part of the family, are you? You never came to stay with us, and I know Maman used to invite you for holidays.'

Brianna bit her lip. 'My grandmother thought it would be too upsetting for me while I was still at school, and after I left she wasn't well, so I was needed there. But of course I want to see my own mother—and you and she are part of my family.'

'Papa was your part of the family—the English part. You're English, Philippe says. I'm French. Me, I don't like the English,' Isabelle added with a frankness that was rude.

Brianna flinched. On the point of remarking that it was rude of Isabelle to express such a narrow-minded attitude, she paused. At roughly Isabelle's age, she had done much the same thing. The fact was, both of them had been brought up with prejudices. Hers had derived from her grandmother. Where had Isabelle's derived from? From the d'Helliers in general? She tried to be fair and not place the bulk of the blame on Philippe, though in her heart she was sure that was where it belonged.

She said briskly, changing the subject, 'I think I'd better go downstairs and fetch my suitcases. And I'm sure Tante Agathe is back. Isn't that a child's voice I can hear?'

'Yes, it's Olympe. She's nearly three and she's never still. It's peaceful when they're all out. Now you're here you'll have to take your turn looking after Micheline's children—Philippe said so.'

Brianna grimaced inwardly—not because she wasn't willing to take her turn, but because that made three times now that Isabelle had quoted Philippe.

Isabelle showed no signs of moving from the bed, and as Brianna crossed to the doorway, she asked, 'Aren't you coming down to introduce me to Tante Agathe?'

Isabelle made a face. 'Philippe said you weren't to be treated like a guest ... You could introduce yourself—you're only my sister, and she knows all about you. If I come down now, I'll be roped into preparing Jean-Christian's bottle, or doing something equally boring.'

Brianna raised her eyebrows and smiled. 'I promise I'll help you then—if you show me what to do.'

'Oh, all right.' Isabelle got to her feet. 'I'd like to take a look at my aperitif, anyhow. It's made from a recipe used by the peasants, you know. It's a lot of fun trying such things out, though Philippe says the results are coarse.'

'Does he?' Brianna commented equably, and asked as

they went down the stairs together, 'Who's Violette? It was she who gave you the recipe, wasn't it?'

'Yes, Violette Dupont. She comes each day to help Tante Agathe in the house. She lives on a farm beyond the village. I'll take you there one day.'

'I'd like that,' Brianna said with a smile. She had the feeling that in a casual way, Isabelle was quite willing to befriend her. She probably remembered very little of her sister's previous visit since at the time she had been wrapped up in her own misery and demanding constant attention from her mother. How she had changed! Now she was the picture of health and self-confidence.

When they reached the big hall at the foot of the stairs, they found Tante Agathe there with the children. She was a thin elderly woman dressed severely in black. Her hair, however, was tinted to almost black, and her face was carefully made up with lipstick and eyeshadow, and she presented an odd sight as she lifted the lustily bawling Jean-Christian—clad in bright orange singlet and matching pants—from his *landau*, while little Olympe, swinging a rag doll by the arm, repeated over and over that she was hungry.

Isabelle made careless introductions in the midst of the clamour, and as they all made their way to the kitchen, Brianna reflected that Philippe's aunt certainly needed some help, with these two infants to be fed and put to bed, and an evening meal to be prepared for the rest of the household. However, she soon discovered that Tante Agathe was a great organiser as well as being an excellent cook, and was endowed with enormous vitality for her age.

'Get Jean-Christian's bottle ready, please, Isabelle,' she ordered, and Isabelle grimaced rudely and said to her sister, 'Come along, Brianna, and I'll help show you what has to be done.'

Tante Agathe sent Brianna a sharp glance. 'You speak French, Brianna?'

'Yes, but not very well. I understand as long as you don't speak too quickly.'

'Good. Then there will be no misunderstandings. Would you like to take Jean-Christian while I deal with Olympe? She'll be a little shy of you at first, despite her noisiness.'

Brianna had taken the brightly clad baby in her arms and was watching Isabelle get his bottle ready when Philippe came into the room with a dark-haired, dark-eyed girl— very vivacious, utterly chic, and utterly French. For a second Brianna thought it must be his girl friend, and then she realised it was Marie-Claude, the girl who had helped to make her life so wretched years ago—the girl she had hated so intensely.

It required a definite effort to say in answer to Philippe's enquiry, 'Yes, of course I remember Marie-Claude', and to turn to the other girl and smile.

Marie-Claude smiled too, but Brianna suspected she was making an effort as well. Deliberately she greeted the d'Hellier girl in French, and saw with satisfaction the way she opened her eyes wide in surprise at the almost faultless accent Brianna had worked so hard to acquire.

She caught Philippe's eye on her, watchful and faintly hostile. 'What have I done now?' she wondered. She discovered what she had done a little later when she took Jean-Christian into the next room to feed him, on Tante Agathe's instructions. It was a living room—a sort of family room, perhaps, big and comfortable. Though it had been re-decorated it still retained much of the atmosphere of a very old house. The walls were of rough stone, the flooring of quarry tiles, and there was a huge old granite fireplace. As far as furniture went, an enormous farm table, sheeny with age, dominated the room. There was an oak sideboard with carved panels, a set of straight-backed chairs, and a long low sofa with a deerskin cover, as well as various other bits of furniture. Double windows and a glass door gave on to the garden, and the light coming in was softened by the green of flowering vines.

Brianna chose a chair and Jean-Christian made an eager attack on his bottle. The world seemed very peaceful, and Brianna relaxed. Marie-Claude had gone upstairs and Isabelle was busy with her aperitif, the strong winey smell of which drifted in from the kitchen.

A minute later her feeling of peace was shattered as Philippe sauntered into the room and stood looking at her narrowly.

'So you speak French these days, do you, Brianna? What was the idea of deceiving me?'

She raised her eyebrows. 'I didn't deceive you. You took it for granted I didn't—just as you take it for granted I'm still the same girl who came to France seven years ago.'

'Not at all,' he contradicted her, his glance flickering over her swiftly. 'I'm fully aware of a number of changes in you. You're a very pretty girl now—you've lost that surplus weight, and you know how to dress. I wondered about that in England, but I see you do know. And you've learnt to move gracefully. But apart from getting it nicely around French vowels, you don't yet appear to be interested in learning grace with your tongue. It's a pity, that. From my experience of you—and I mean *this* time—I'd say this is a decidedly armed truce.'

'From my experience of you,' she retorted, altering the position of her arm under the baby's head, 'I'd guess *you're* prepared to fire a few threatening shots past my ears just to remind me I still belong to the enemy camp. I've heard the odd bullet whining past already.'

'Have you?' He smiled slightly. 'You've expressed yourself very well, anyhow——'

'For an English girl?' she put in swiftly.

'Well, I hadn't intended to qualify that remark, but if you want it that way—yes, you've expressed yourself very well for someone using a foreign tongue ... All the same, I don't think my threatening shots have frightened you much, have they?'

'No, they haven't,' she agreed, looking straight up at him, her eyes wide.

He laughed lightly. 'When you look at me like that, Brianna, you almost persuade me to throw away my arms! But I've met plenty of other girls whose eyes make daring statements, and I've learned long ago not to believe them. Save your eye language for your English fiancé, at all events, and count on it that I'm going to hang on to my ammunition and that I'll certainly use it if necessary.'

'That *is* a threat,' she said. 'But I don't know what it's all about. Do you plan to make life unpleasant for me for some reason?'

'That depends on how you behave. Haven't you found it generally to be the way?' he added dryly, referring, she supposed, to her last sojourn in his country. 'But be sure of one thing, you won't leave here until I say the word, fiancé or no fiancé. I've already told you why. When I write to Switzerland, I want to be able to say that you're among us and that amicable relations have been established. That way, your mother's mind will be at rest.'

Brianna felt a hot resentment rise up in her. Philippe was as good as telling her he didn't believe she had good intentions regarding her French relatives, and she told him abruptly, 'I'll do as I think best about staying here. And don't bother telling me I'm already behaving badly by speaking to my host this way. Just remember you're the one who's chosen to treat me as some kind of enemy prisoner.'

'You want to make a melodrama of it, do you?' he said.

'*You* do,' she retorted.

They stared at each other for a moment and then he turned his back and walked away.

Brianna gently took the bottle from Jean-Christian and

held him against her shoulder, rubbing his back a little the way Peter's sister had showed her to do. Her mind was preoccupied with the conversation that had just ended, and she felt troubled. Who had started the hostilities just now? She thought it was Philippe, but admittedly she was only too ready to defend herself—and to attack as well. It was a great pity he couldn't forget the past and try to believe in her good intentions, and she rather suspected that the fact that she was English was at the base of it. She didn't think she had much chance of winning *him* over, and truth to tell she wasn't particularly inclined to try. He was so didactic, so keen on giving her orders—'You won't leave here until I say so, fiancé or no fiancé.' Oh dear, Mrs Arden must really have given him an earful about the relationship between herself and Peter! Well, he could think what he pleased about that, she didn't care...

In the kitchen, Olympe was reluctantly sitting at a small table and eating her supper.

'She eats with her parents at home in Dijon,' Tante Agathe said disapprovingly. 'But here we do things my way, Olympe. Our meal is going to be late and you'll be too tired to enjoy your good food if you wait until then. Already you're yawning like an owl. Where's Isabelle?' she asked Brianna. 'She must change baby and put him to bed and not leave everything to you on your first evening with us. Marie-Claude will look after Olympe presently, she's gone into the garden to fetch me some parsley. We'll have omelettes tonight.'

Brianna escaped from what seemed an unending flow of French to find Isabelle, who turned out to be upstairs in her room rearranging her hair. She had undone her plaits and now her hair was brushed out around her face, making her look prettier than ever. Not pleased at Brianna's interruption, she snatched the child and carried him off to the nursery.

'Tante Agathe needn't think I'm going to do this every night now you're here,' she said ungratefully.

The evening meal was not served till a good hour later. It was a noisy gathering, for both Tante Agathe and Isabelle were great talkers. Brianna was quite exhausted trying to follow the conversation and had given up long before the meal was finished.

'Please make the coffee, Isabelle,' Tante Agathe ordered, and Isabelle tossed back her hair and complained, 'I don't make such good coffee as Marie-Claude.'

'Come, come—do as you're told,' Tante Agathe said briskly, and Brianna thought, 'Those two don't hit it off terribly well'. She followed her sister out of the room with a murmured excuse and helped her, and later at the table asked quietly, 'Shall I do the dishes?'

'Violette will do those in the morning,' Tante Agathe explained.

'*Dieu merci*,' remarked Isabelle. 'Otherwise *I'd* be the one to do them, even though it's my holiday. Marie-Claude only works when it pleases her.'

'Oh, *tais-toi*,' Tante Agathe said. 'You must learn to play your part in family life. You don't come down from Paris to play about from morning till night. Tomorrow morning you can do the shopping for me while I start preparations for dinner. I had Violette bring me a nice chicken from the farm,' she added, turning to Philippe who was sitting back in his chair smoking, and saying little.

'Excellent,' he said, and added dryly, 'We must have a little celebration to welcome Brianna. And when the shopping's done,' he continued, looking at Isabelle through narrowed eyes, 'you and your sister can put your heads together over some English books. You're to do at least an hour of study and conversation every morning while you're here. It will keep you—both of you—out of mischief.'

Isabelle merely pouted, but Brianna felt her cheeks flame

and she itched to make some fiery objection. She didn't like having her time ordered for her this way, and neither did she like being talked to as if she were a child. She was far too old for that. Unable to hold the words back, she exclaimed angrily, 'Isabelle and I can talk together in English any time during the day. Tante Agathe will need our help in the mornings.'

'Oh, not at all, not at all,' Tante Agathe said soothingly. 'I have Violette to help me in the mornings. It's an admirable arrangement.'

Philippe got up from the table and sent Brianna a sardonic look of triumph.

'Then that's decided,' he said flatly, and left the room.

CHAPTER THREE

NEVERTHELESS, the English lessons didn't proceed exactly according to plan. The idea of sitting down for an hour—Philippe had allotted them the table on the landing as the official place for study—and making a lesson of it didn't appeal to Brianna at all. Nor, quite obviously, did it appeal to Isabelle.

However, Tante Agathe had a great respect for her nephew's commands and she took it upon herself to urge Isabelle up the stairs while diplomatically taking it for granted that Brianna would comply with her stepbrother's wishes without having to be prodded into it. Isabelle went grumblingly, muttering angrily, 'I'm not a child five years old to be told what I must do,' and she wasted all the time in the world finding books, and openly admitted that she didn't care a cent about becoming proficient in English.

At the second 'lesson', rather surprisingly, Marie-Claude put in an appearance, and asked apologetically, 'Do you mind if I sit and listen, Brianna? My English is not good and I should like to improve it.'

'You're welcome,' Brianna said pleasantly. Neither she nor her stepsister had referred to the feud that had existed between them in the past, and in fact they had very little to say to one another so far, but it was over the so-called lesson that the two girls began to communicate with each other, while Isabelle lounged back in her chair idly, allowing her attention to wander where it would.

Marie-Claude wanted to know if Brianna lived far from London.

'Not very far,' Brianna told her obligingly. 'I live in Kent

—in Canterbury. It's a very lovely cathedral city—not far from Dover. I go up to London now and again.'

'I should like to go there. I have seen many photographs, and it is not like Paris. Paris I love, but I should like to visit London.'

Brianna felt vaguely surprised. She hadn't thought England would interest Marie-Claude in the slightest—but now it was she who was judging her on a past that was well and truly outgrown.

'You could go there for your honeymoon,' said Isabelle slyly, sitting up and taking notice, and the other girl coloured furiously.

'Are you engaged, Marie-Claude?' Brianna asked politely.

Marie-Claude didn't answer, but Isabelle hugged her knees and said, 'She will be soon—to Louis Moreau. It's all been arranged. And now Madame Hubert-Benoise is hard at work on Philippe and Albertine.'

'That's enough,' Marie-Claude said sharply. 'None of these things are—are certain. Besides, you mustn't discuss Philippe's affairs with—with anyone at all.'

Brianna ignored the remark, but she felt it was a little slighting. After all, she was supposed to be part of the family. Still, the fact was, she wasn't, and no one was more aware of it than herself, but all the same she felt a deep stirring of curiosity. It was Madame Hubert-Benoise who owned the manor house and the vineyards on the outskirts of the village, she remembered, and she would have liked to ask who Louis Moreau was, and Albertine, and what they had to do with Madame Hubert-Benoise, but pride forbade it. Possibly if Marie-Claude had not been there, Isabelle would have gone on chattering about family affairs—she was a real chatterbox, that much Brianna had learned in a very short time. As it was, Marie-Claude changed the direction of the conversation.

'You have a boy-friend in England, Brianna?'

'Oh, I've had several boy-friends. Nothing serious, though.'

'To whom were you writing your letters last night?' Marie-Claude was so careful and correct with her grammar that Brianna wanted to laugh. It somehow made the question sound polite rather than impertinent, and she quickly suppressed her smile as the other girl asked, her pride hurt, 'You find my accent comical?'

'No, of course not. I was—I was just smiling to think how surprised Mrs Arden—to whom I was writing—will be to find I'm not in Paris after all, but in the country,' she improvised hastily. 'She envied my going to Paris, you see —she spent a little time there herself, some years ago.'

'I understand.' Marie-Claude sounded aloof and not totally convinced, and Isabelle said, staring hard at her sister, 'You wrote two letters. I saw the names on the envelopes and the other one was to Peter Arden. Is he your boy-friend?'

Now it was Brianna who coloured, and she said with a touch of annoyance, 'I've told you, I have several boy-friends.' She turned back to Marie-Claude. 'What kind of work do you do? Do you have to earn a living?'

'But no! Since school is finished, I work sometimes for Paul in Dijon. Since our uncle has died, he manages that branch of our—our wine shipping company,' she finished triumphantly. 'Sometimes I stay in Paris with my father and my *belle-mère*, and sometimes I stay here with Tante Agathe and Philippe.'

'Marie-Claude likes very much the country,' Isabelle offered with an innocent air. '*Parce que* 'er boy-friend is in Huchet-les-Anges. Madame Hubert-Benoise is 'is *grand'-mère*. You would like to meet 'im, Brianna?'

'Yes, of course,' said Brianna, but Marie-Claude didn't take it up, and that subject was dropped too. She supposed a little wryly that she was not considered sufficiently 'family' for it to warrant a special visit and an introduction.

At all events, when, the following day, Marie-Claude set off for Les Charmes, she didn't invite Brianna to accompany her.

Philippe came home during the afternoon. Isabelle was washing her hair, the two children and Tante Agathe were all asleep in the summer heat. Brianna was alone in the living room, and looked up from the couch where she was sitting glancing through some of Olympe's picture books and coloured when she saw it was Philippe who had come in.

'Tante Agathe and the children are sleeping,' she said unnecessarily.

He took a chair opposite her, stretched out his legs and looked at her curiously. 'Tell me what you've been doing with yourself, Brianna.'

He looked slightly weary, she thought, and somehow aggressively French today. 'Aristocratic' was the word that came into her mind—rather incongruously, because he was casually dressed in jeans and matching shirt of fine blue denim. It was the first time she had been alone with him since the evening of her arrival, and she felt as nervous as a student who has been singled out to give an address on a subject she hasn't prepared. She swallowed and said casually, 'I haven't been doing anything particularly interesting.'

'You're bored?'

'I didn't say that. I meant—nothing you'd be interested to hear about.'

'You make an error, my little *belle-soeur*. Anything you've been doing interests me.'

'Really? Then I suppose you'll be fascinated to know that today I made up the formula for Jean-Christian's bottle, that I read Olympe a story and—let's see—— Oh yes, I showed her what is in every little pot and jar on my dressing table, and the picture on the back of my hand-mirror. I also had quite a conversation with Violette, and learned that her father makes a wine that compares very favourably with any of yours.'

His dark eyebrows rose. 'Is that your opinion or Violette's?'

'Which do you think?' she asked, flushing angrily, 'I know her father's a peasant—that he makes a very rough wine. I'll agree I'm not a connoisseur when it comes to wine, but I think you're being deliberately insulting. Aren't you?'

'No,' he said, bringing his fingers together under his chin and looking at her with concentration. 'I thought, however, that that was *your* object. It seems we've misunderstood each other. I apologise.'

Brianna said nothing. Somehow she couldn't make herself offer an apology of her own. She felt distinctly ruffled, and she was convinced Philippe had a poor enough opinion of her taste to have meant what he had seemed to imply.

'Where's Isabelle?' he asked after a minute.

'Upstairs washing her hair.'

'And my sister?'

'She's gone to Les Charmes to see—someone.'

'She didn't invite you to go with her?'

'No.'

'Aren't you two getting on together?'

'Oh, we're scraping along very amicably,' she said dryly. 'We didn't like each other at all when first we met, you know.'

'You didn't like any of us, did you?'

'Nor did any of you like me,' she retorted. Any idea she'd had of mentioning that she and Marie-Claude had been getting together over language lessons went by the board.

'Isabelle's improving at her English?' he asked, ignoring her remark.

She shrugged. 'You'll have to judge that for yourself.'

He looked at her for a moment, then moved restlessly and stood up. 'I'm going to Armette to see the jeweller and attend to some business.' He paused and looked at her very assessingly, seeming to take in every detail of her dress. She was wearing a pale blue blouse with a round neck, and a simple, slightly flared darker blue skirt with a narrow tie at the waistband—one of the outfits she had bought especially to bring to France. She knew she looked cool and fresh except for her still burning cheeks, and she hoped rather wryly that he approved, but his next words surprised her. 'Would you like to come with me, little *belle-soeur*?'

She stared at him incredulously as if he had suggested something utterly preposterous—as in a way he had, for she never expected to receive any sort of invitation from him.

'Me?' she stammered. 'What for?'

His mouth lifted at one corner in a derisive smile. 'I'm not inviting you to come to the jewellers, *ma petite*, simply to Armette. You might like to do some shopping, or you might simply come for the drive, seeing you're at a loose end.'

'But—Tante Agathe—the children——'

'Oh, Isabelle's here. You've been industrious enough for one day, a break will surely be welcome ... Well?'

'Oh yes, I'll come,' she agreed after a slight hesitation, and almost immediately wished she had refused. It seemed in a curious way to be a lowering of the flag to agree so tamely to doing what he suggested. 'I'll just slip upstairs and——'

'No,' he broke in. 'You don't need to go upstairs for anything. Your appearance is faultless—you're a true English rose today. If you need any money, I shall lend you some. There'll only be problems if Isabelle discovers what's going on. She'll want to come too and I intend to leave immediately. Besides, someone must be here to help Tante Agathe.'

'Perhaps I should stay,' Brianna began, but he reached over and took the story book from her lap and held it up mockingly.

'I know you don't particularly care for my company, but I shall be really insulted if you pretend I'm less stimulating than this kind of thing!'

Brianna gave in.

It was pleasant driving back along the road they had taken when they came down from Paris, and she leaned back in the car and let the fresh air blow in on her face through the open window of the Citroën. It was good to get away from the house for a while. She had been under quite a little strain there in various ways, not all of them connected with Philippe, who at any rate wasn't bothering her now, but simply let her relax in silence. Presently she began to think of what he had said about going to the jeweller's in Armette. Putting two and two together—the jeweller, plus the girl called Albertine, whom Isabelle had mentioned—she made four, which was a romance. She glanced cautiously at the man beside her, and reflected that at thirty-three or four it was certainly time he was not only engaged but married. He had a pleasant profile, she decided, strong yet softened just now at any rate by the agreeable curve where his lips met. She supposed that to a French girl he could be very attractive, very desirable even. He looked good and he was obviously well off. Today's English conversation class had brought forth the information that his maternal grandfather had left Les Fleurons to him, and that as well he was the chairman of a syndicate which owned several vineyards in the district. Plainly Isabelle's remark that Madame Hubert-Benoise was 'hard at work' on Philippe and Albertine meant that she wanted them to marry, and she longed to ask him who Albertine was. However, she could hardly do so with an abrupt question, and she thought a little frustratedly that it was odd to be part of a family yet know so little of their personal lives.

In the midst of her reflections, Philippe asked her, 'Have you heard from your fiancé yet?'

She raised her eyebrows. 'If you mean Peter Arden—no.'

'Well, of course I mean Peter Arden. Who else would I mean? You surely can have only one fiancé at a time.'

'Yes, but I don't happen to be engaged to Peter Arden or to anyone else,' she said stiffly.

'I've noticed you wear no ring,' he agreed. 'And I'm aware formal engagements are disregarded by the young these days, but Mrs Arden made the situation very clear ... However, if you don't care to discuss your personal affairs with me, we'll forget it.'

'Thank you,' she said sarcastically, and couldn't resist adding, 'Don't you know the English are supposed to be reticent? It's supposed to be the French who tell you every intimate detail of their private lives the moment they meet you. Not that I've noticed it with the d'Helliers—at least so far as *I'm* concerned.'

'You sound disappointed. What is it you want to know? Something about me?' He cast her a quick look and discovered her flushing. He went on smoothly, 'I'm not married, not engaged. I don't have a mistress—though I suppose *you* believe every Frenchman has a mistress. Will that suffice?'

'Perfectly,' she said, her cheeks still red, and added simply to disconcert him, 'I wasn't thinking of you, as a matter of fact. I was thinking of Marie-Claude.'

His only reaction was a slight frown. 'I'm sure she's not trying to keep anything from you. It's possible she'll soon become engaged, but until it happens there's no sense in discussing it, is there? It's her affair entirely ... I gather Isabelle's been gossiping.'

'Well, she hasn't been,' she said, feeling annoyed on her sister's behalf. 'Anything she said was in front of Marie-Claude.'

'You needn't defend her. We all know tactfulness isn't one of Isabelle's virtues. What has she been telling you in the way of family secrets?'

'Nothing. But I concluded that the—the family are trying to arrange the match,' she continued rashly.

'Well, rest assured that no one will expect Marie-Claude to marry anyone she doesn't love. Though even love,' he added after a moment, 'is no guarantee of happiness, and a marriage based on it can still end in disaster.'

'I know that,' she said, her voice low. She was thinking of her own parents. Actually, no one had ever talked to her sympathetically about her parents' marriage, because her grandmother had been terribly prejudiced, a fact she had only begun to appreciate after she grew up, but she felt sure theirs had been a love match, even though they had become totally estranged from each other.

'In fact,' Philippe was saying, 'there's quite a lot to be said for marriages arranged by the families concerned. I'd be the last one to damn them.'

They had reached Armette now and were driving along a wide street by gardens with gilded iron gates, a pool, a white marble statue. Philippe made a right-hand turn and drove into a large parking area.

'My business will take me about an hour,' he said, then climbed out of the car and came round to the other side to see her out too. 'Here.' He pulled out his wallet and handed her some notes. 'Take this in case your window-shopping has you frustrated.'

She put her hands behind her back. 'No, thank you.'

'Now don't be touchy about it. I know exactly how much is there—a hundred francs, if you're curious. It's very little, and you can return it once we're home again.'

'I don't need it,' she said stubbornly, then at the look in his eye added reluctantly, 'Very well, I'll take ten francs. All I'm likely to want is a cool drink or a cup of coffee.' She took the wad of notes, handed him back the bulk of it, then folded the ten francs she had kept and tucked it carelessly with her handkerchief into her belt, and together they walked towards the main street.

'We'll have a drink together later,' said Philippe. 'I'll meet you outside the café opposite. You can sit down at one of the pavement tables if you have to wait and I'll do the same ... One hour, then.'

She nodded and they parted company.

Brianna walked slowly, presently crossing the street to the shady side, where she looked into the shop windows. Armette appeared to be quite a prosperous town, and the shop windows were attractive. She noticed that several shops were closed for the month of August, but there was plenty to look at and it was entertaining simply to watch the people, to listen to the quick lively French conversation, and to feel herself, somehow for the first time, actually in France, amongst people who were so totally different from the English. She wondered fleetingly if her own French blood were stirred in some mysterious way as she wandered alone along the busy street.

Presently she went into a Prisunic supermarket and sauntered about, staring at all the unfamiliar goods on the shelves with their French packaging, examining the yoghurts and cheeses in a big refrigerated storage case. She'd heard somewhere that there was supposed to be a different cheese for every day of the year in France, and she could well believe it as she looked at all the fascinating varieties. Camemberts with exotic and fanciful names—a peppered Boursin like the one Tante Agathe had put on the table last night—

It was all quite novel to Brianna, but she left the super-

market without buying anything, then decided, seeing she
still had a half hour before it was time to meet Philippe,
that perhaps she'd buy some sweets for Olympe. She found
a confectionery shop and stood looking at the elaborately
decorated window where there were elegantly boxed and
arranged chocolates and bonbons and fruit jellies. The
prices were high, but ten francs would buy a minute box
of jellies—made from pure fruits, she translated. That
would be better for Olympe than chocolate, anyhow.

Inside the shop there were two other customers—a rather
opulently dressed woman who was just being handed a
large box, tissue wrapped and decorated with a great curl of
gold satin ribbon. The other customer was a young man
with very blond hair, who was being attended to by a
second assistant.

When her turn came, Brianna explained in careful French
what she wanted, and as she did so the young man turned
his head and smiled at her as if he knew her. She blinked
slightly and glanced away. He must be trying to pick her up,
and while that might be amusing, she simply hadn't the time
to be picked up today. The thought amused her still more,
but her half suppressed smile soon vanished as, groping in
her belt for the money she had tucked in it with her handkerchief, she discovered it simply wasn't there.

Oh, heavens! How frightful! It must have slipped out
somewhere along the line. She watched with a sort of awful
fascination as the shop assistant returned to the counter
with her box of jellies and fastidiously wrapped it in pink
tissue. Silvery ribbon was produced, and in a matter of
seconds a charming rosette of curls and loops had been
fabricated.

Brianna swallowed nervously. There was nothing else to
do but admit that she had lost her money, and she felt an
absolute fool. Her mind seemed to have gone blank as re-

gards the French language, and she was trying to put words together in her mind when the blond young man, who had not yet left the shop, asked her in a voice that was definitely English, 'What's the matter? Lost your pocket?'

'My—my pocket?' she repeated, staring.

'Your money purse, then,' he said with a grin. 'I was being tactful—adding the lighter touch ... Have you?'

She smiled back at him a little doubtfully. 'I have, as a matter of fact. At least, it's just ten francs. I'd tucked it into my belt, rather stupidly—'

'Well, don't worry.' He fished in his pocket, produced the required money and handed it across the counter to the slightly disapproving assistant, and in another minute they were walking out of the shop together, both of them laughing.

'I'll pay it back,' said Brianna. 'Can you wait about twenty minutes?'

He looked at her seriously and she looked back at him, thinking how utterly nice he was and how marvellous it was to be talking in English to an Englishman again.

'I can wait much longer than that—if you'll have coffee with me.'

'I'd love to,' she said honestly.

'There's a good little pavement café nearby—we'll go there.'

'You're English', she remarked unnecessarily as they made their way back along the street to the place, as it turned out, where she was to meet Philippe. 'That was why you smiled at me, of course. I thought you were—trying to pick me up.'

'Oh, I was,' he assured her humorously. 'And I managed it too, didn't I?'

'Luckily for me,' she agreed. 'Do you live in France? You speak the language so perfectly—'

'I was brought up bi-lingual. My mother's French. My home's in England, actually—my name's Richard Hazelwood, by the way.'

'I'm Brianna Gaze.'

They had reached the tables and he found one that was unoccupied. They sat down opposite each other in the shade of a red sun umbrella, that had faded to rose in the summer sun. They smiled across at each other, and looked at each other curiously, and Brianna enjoyed the slight sexiness in his blue-grey eyes that told her he found her attractive. He ordered two coffees, and she listened to his voice and approved both that and his good-looking very English face, and the fair hair that fell across his forehead and brushed the collar of his open-necked, mushroom-pink shirt.

'What are you doing in Armette?' he asked when the waiter had darted off. 'Holidaying? You're not an *au pair* girl, by any chance?'

She shook her head. 'I was just looking round the shops. I came over with my stepbrother from Huchet-les-Anges. Do you know it? It's a rather small village.'

His laugh surprised her. 'Of course I know it! I've been living there with my grandmother for the past seven weeks. Who's your stepbrother?'

'Philippe d'Hellier. My mother is married to his father.'

'Good lord!' he exclaimed, then, when the waiter had brought the coffee, 'I've met him, of course. And Marie-Claude,' he added, stirring sugar into his coffee.

Brianna looked at him through her lashes. She wasn't sure if his tone expressed approval of the d'Helliers or otherwise. There was a certain—guarded note in it, she thought. She told him lightly, 'Well, I don't expect I know your grandmother. I haven't met anyone in the village in the short time I've been there. Is she French or English?'

'French—and how! To the last cubic centimetre. Do you know the old manor house this end of Huchet?'

'Yes, of course,' Brianna said with a slight start of surprise. 'It looks very impressive.'

'It does, doesn't it? It's certainly huge—but it's very old. It needs a new roof and the central heating's packing up, and there are so many repairs and renovations crying out to be done one could fill a book with them. Trouble is, there's not the money. Grand'mère—Madame Hubert-Benoise to you—possesses only one vineyard—that's Les Charmes. It doesn't produce top quality wines, so there's never been very much money. I used to go there with my mother for holidays sometimes when I was a kid—Mother was the bad daughter who married an Englishman. I hadn't been back for ages until this year. I've been earning a living, you know, and it does cut down on holiday time. My father's a paint manufacturer and as the eldest son I'm expected to take an interest in the business, but I'm afraid the only kind of paints that really interest me are oil paints. I have ambitions in the artistic line.'

'Really? Are you going to study in Paris?'

'No such luck. I attended night classes at home, and now my father's released me from bondage for twelve months so I can find out what stuff I'm made of. This summer, I thought why not seek inspiration in fair France and impose myself on Grand'mère. 'She won't tolerate you,' my father said. She doesn't like the English, you see. But my mother seemed to think I might win her round, and I suppose I have in a way. She loves me a little and despises my English character a lot, but all in all she tolerates me as a kind of folly,' he added with a charming grin. 'However, if I don't watch it I'll be more of a folly than she can tolerate ... My God, I *am* running on about myself, aren't I? Let's talk about you for a change. You can't have been in Huchet for long or I'd have heard something about you from Albertine for sure.'

Albertine! The name made Brianna's nerves leap, though

why she couldn't think. She sipped her cooling coffee, leaned her elbows on the table and looked at Richard Hazelwood enquiringly.

'No, I haven't been here long. But you've got me confused. Who's Albertine?'

'My cousin, Albertine Moreau. Her mother's the *good* daughter who married a Frenchman. Bertine lives with her parents here in Armette. My uncle André is a solicitor and she works for him. She comes to Huchet for a weekend every so often. Grand'mère has Louis fetch her in the car. And Louis,' he explained, seeing her raised eyebrows, 'is her brother. He manages the vineyards for Grand'mère. He's an admirable character—very French.'

'You don't like him much?' she suggested with a slight smile.

'Oh, I like him—he's great.' Richard shrugged his slim shoulders and said no more, and it was Brianna who said recklessly, 'I believe he and my stepsister Marie-Claude are close friends.'

His rather long eyelashes flicked up and his eyes met hers expressionlessly. 'That's right ... Do you want some more coffee?'

She glanced at her watch. 'I'd better not. Philippe will be here any time now. I was supposed to meet him here for a drink.'

'As you please. Is—Marie-Claude with him?'

'No. She went to visit your grandmother this afternoon.'

'Oh? I didn't know she was expected, though I should have guessed. I was despatched to do some shopping—and as well I needed a couple of tubes of paint. Well, I won't wait till Philippe comes.'

'But you must,' she said with a laugh. 'I owe you ten francs!'

'Oh, you can pay that back any time. Now I know you're

Take this superb volume
FREE!

Lucy Gillen sets this romance among the wild lochs and mountains of Scotland. **"A Wife for Andrew"** is a touching account of a young governess, her dour yet compassionate employer and the children in his care who suffer at the hands of a jealous woman.

In Betty Neels' **"Fate Is Remarkable"** Sarah's "marriage of convenience" is dramatically altered. Just as Sarah was getting ready to tell Hugo that she'd fallen in love with him, a lovely woman from Hugo's past shows up . . .

In **"Bitter Masquerade"** by Margery Hilton, mistaken identity is the basis of Virginia Dalmont's marriage. When Brent mistook her for her twin sister Anna, she wondered if her love was strong enough to make up for the deceit. . .

In the pages of your FREE GIFT Romance Treasury Volume you'll get to know warm, true-to-life people, and you'll discover the special kind of miracle that love can be. The stories will sweep you to distant lands where intrigue, adventure and the destiny of many lives will thrill you. All three full-length novels are exquisitely bound together in a single hardcover volume that's your FREE GIFT, to introduce you to Harlequin Romance Treasury!

The most beautiful books you've ever seen!
Cover and spine of all volumes feature distinctive gilt designs. And an elegant bound-in ribbon bookmark adds a lovely feminine touch. No detail has been overlooked to make Romance Treasury books as beautiful and lasting as the stories they contain. What a delightful way to enjoy the very best and most popular Harlequin romances again and again!

A whole world of romantic adventures!
If you are delighted with your FREE GIFT volume, you may, if you wish, receive a new Harlequin Romance Treasury volume as published every five weeks or so — delivered right to your door! The beautiful FREE GIFT VOLUME is yours to keep with no obligation to buy anything.

Fill out the coupon today to receive your FREE GIFT VOLUME.

Romance Treasury
from Harlequin

Three exciting, full length Romance novels in one beautiful book ...

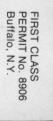

in Huchet, you must come over to the manor one day—see my famous paintings—'

'I'd like that,' she said enthusiastically, though her enthusiasm was part curiosity.

'I'll have to check with Grand'mère before I invite you, I'm afraid. She's a rather formal old dear—doesn't altogether approve of my casual English ways. I have to watch it ... You speak good French, by the way—she'll like *that*. Are you a hundred per cent English or a fifty-fifty mixture like me? I can't imagine the d'Helliers with an English stepmother.'

'No, my mother's French. But I wasn't brought up bilingual like you. I have to think hard before I say anything at all complicated. I've really enjoyed talking English to you.'

'What do you do with yourself all day?'

Brianna was about to tell him about the children, and the English lessons, but at that precise moment Philippe appeared. Brianna thought he didn't look altogether pleased to see her sitting at the table with a young man. Richard stood up at once and the two men greeted each other rather formally, and Richard didn't sit down again.

'If you'll excuse me, I must go ... I'll be in touch with you, Brianna.'

She let him go without mentioning the ten francs again. She could easily repay it later—and privately. She didn't particularly want Philippe to know she had been so careless as to lose the money she had accepted from him.

'You've had coffee already,' he remarked rather coldly.

'Only one tiny cup,' she said offhandedly. 'I could easily drink another—that is, if you're having any.'

'I am.' He asked the waiter for two cups, then remarked, narrowing his very blue eyes, 'I wasn't aware you'd met Richard Hazelwood.'

'I hadn't. We met just now.'

'You mean he picked you up?'

She shrugged. 'I suppose you could say that.'

'And you let him?'

'Obviously. But why not? He's English.'

Philippe raised his eyes heavenwards. '*Mon dieu*! You mean you'd let any man pick you up provided he's English?'

'Of course I don't! But I thought he looked nice, and anyhow, what could possibly happen to me sitting at this table?' she asked, half annoyed, half amused.

'He asked to share your table, did he?'

She hesitated, then with a sigh said 'No. Actually we met at the confectioners—we struck up a conversation because we're both English.' She changed the subject swiftly. 'Did you see the jeweller and complete your other business?'

'Yes,' he said abruptly, quickly drinking down the coffee that had been brought to them a few moments ago. 'I had to see my lawyer, Monsieur Moreau.'

'And Albertine, who works for him,' she thought instantly. 'I bought some sweets for Olympe,' she said aloud. 'I'll repay your ten francs when we get home.'

'Don't worry too much about it,' he said dryly. 'Shall we go?'

As they walked the short distance to the car park, he asked her, 'Have you enjoyed your afternoon?'

'Very much. It was fun talking to someone English again.'

He raised his eyebrows. 'It amuses me to hear you repeatedly calling Madame Hubert-Benoise's grandson English. I'm afraid she wouldn't like it.' They reached the car and as he climbed in beside her she said argumentatively, 'I'd still call him English rather than French. Besides, you consider *me* English, don't you?'

He turned his head and looked at her piercingly. 'Completely,' he agreed.

She felt her usual surge of frustration and mild fury at

his manner. 'Then Richard's English too. At any rate, I like him.'

'Not too much, it's to be hoped. Seeing you have an admirer waiting for you in England.'

'For goodness' sake!' she exclaimed, as he drove out of the parking area. 'There's such a thing as a platonic friendship, you know.'

She saw his lip curl. 'It's a thing I don't believe in. What Frenchman does?'

'Well, Richard's not French.'

'He's half French. He was well aware of your sex from the minute he spoke to you, I should imagine. Wasn't he, now?'

'I didn't notice,' she said coldly. But she had noticed— she had even taken pleasure in the slightly sexy way he had looked at her. In other words, her own feelings hadn't been of the purely platonic variety either.

'You're going to see him again, of course.'

'Yes. You're not going to tell me it's not allowed, I hope.'

'I wouldn't dream of interfering. You must conduct your love life as you see fit. Only I hope you won't indulge in a flirtation out of sheer boredom, and finish up in a situation you'll want to escape.'

'I'm afraid I can't see that it should matter to you anyway. It's not the sort of thing that will affect your—report on me when you write to Maman, surely.'

'No. But I'd naturally prefer you to keep out of situations you want to escape from. The whole idea is that you stay among us, establishing good relationships. Remember?'

'Don't worry, I haven't forgotten,' she said. 'But you don't help much, do you? You find fault with me every time we exchange a couple of sentences.'

'Do I? That could be because I'm having difficulty in overcoming my prejudices. You were such an objectionable girl last time you came to stay.'

'Thank you,' she said tensely. 'It's good of you to remind

me of it so constantly. It's not something I should be allowed to forget, is it?'

'It's not a performance you should be allowed to repeat,'
he amended it.

'As if I would!' she muttered angrily. She slumped back
in the seat and gazed out the window. What a stupid, futile
conversation! Would he never stop harping on her past
misdemeanours? No one, as far as she knew, ever reminded
Marie-Claude of how beastly *she* had been all those years
ago. But then of course Marie-Claude was *French*—to the
last cubic centimetre, as Richard Hazelwood would put it.
The thought of him made her cheer up. It was going to be
pleasant to have a friend outside the family in Huchet—an
English friend at that. *She* chose to call him English, anyhow. Actually, the only real fly in the ointment was Philippe.
But for him, she could be perfectly content, perfectly at ease
in Huchet-les-Anges. There'd be no problems at all. Any
impossible situation she might want to escape from would
be caused by him—not by her friendship with Richard
Hazelwood, she was convinced of it.

It was a conviction that proved later to be all too true,
though not in the way she imagined it!

CHAPTER FOUR

A DAY or so later Marie-Claude remarked casually, in the course of an English conversation from which Isabelle had disappeared with some trumped-up excuse, that she and Philippe had been invited to the manor by Madame Hubert-Benoise. They were to go at five, and to stay to dinner.

Brianna's immediate reaction was surprise and disappointment that she hadn't been included too. To cover her feeling, she asked brightly, 'Is it going to be a dinner party?'

'Oh no, it's a family affair. Louis will be there—and Albertine, of course.'

'And Richard Hazelwood?' Brianna couldn't stop herself asking. She hadn't told either Marie-Claude or Isabelle about meeting Richard in Armette, possibly because Philippe hadn't referred to it. But as well, there had been no occasion on which the topic had arisen naturally, but now it had. And she could see that Marie-Claude was the one who was surprised this time. She even dropped her pen, and stooping to pick it up, she remarked, 'I didn't know you had met Richard, Brianna. Perhaps when you took Olympe for a walk one day you encountered him sketching in the village?'

'No. I met him the day I went to Armette with Philippe.'

'You didn't mention it before, Brianna.'

'I didn't think anyone would be particularly interested in what happened to me that day in Armette.'

Marie-Claude's eyes fell. 'We leave you out of the conversation at the table. I'm sorry ... I've met Richard several times. Did he tell you we were acquainted?'

'Yes. He said he'd met both you and Philippe. We—we met by chance in the *confiserie*, as a matter of fact. He noticed my English accent.'

'You haven't seen him since?'

'Not yet. But he's promised to ask me to the manor. I'd like to see his paintings.'

'Oh yes ... Now if you don't mind, I think I've had enough English for today and there are things I want to do. Please excuse me.' They smiled at each other, and Marie-Claude picked up her notebook and went.

Brianna frowned thoughtfully. There was still a distance between them that seemed impossible to bridge. She wandered along to her bedroom—the 'room for friends'. Was she a friend? No, she was a guest. She didn't really fit into this French family of her mother's, and it was a blow that she hadn't been invited out to dinner tonight. She stood rather disconsolately in the middle of the room looking across at her reflection in the wall mirror. In contrast to Marie-Claude, whose vivid, lively face had been opposite her for the past hour, she looked very pale and colourless, she thought critically. Such indeterminate hair and eyes. Her mouth too big, her body too slim, and lacking the very feminine curves of her smaller, younger stepsister. An English rose, Philippe had said the other day, she suddenly remembered, and saw the colour unexpectedly flame in her cheeks, so that she turned away. She couldn't see much of the English rose about herself. A few prickles, maybe. Yes, she was feeling decidedly prickly today.

She sat down absentmindedly on the side of the bed and found she was wondering what Albertine Moreau was like. Albertine would be at the manor, 'of course', as Marie-Claude had said. But why of course, since she lived in Armette? Because Philippe would be there? Because Madame Hubert-Benoise was hard at work on Philippe and Albertine? Did Philippe mind this or was he agreeable? He'd said he quite approved of family arrangements. And undoubtedly his money would help to pay for all the work that should be done on the manor, according to Richard.

But what was there in it for him? The manor itself? Or was he, quite simply, in love with Albertine Moreau?

Brianna rose restlessly and wandered to the window. The English lesson had been late this morning because poor Olympe was suffering from insect bites. It was the *aoûtat*, Tante Agathe said. So tiny, so impossible to detect, so rife in the month of August, after which it was named. Isabelle had been sent to the chemist in the village for some lotion to soothe the bites, and she had taken her time about returning.

Now Brianna saw Violette wheel her bicycle out through the big iron gates, then ride off along the narrow road away from the village. She was a pleasant girl with a rather stolid expression and a very respectful attitude towards Tante Agathe. Brianna found her rough country accent a little hard to understand, so she hadn't talked to her very much. She was a peasant—the French still called people peasants.

Albertine, the thought followed naturally, was not a peasant. Probably she was soignée, sophisticated, chic—all the things a French girl should be. Just the sort of wife for a man like Philippe d'Hellier, who of course would never dream of marrying anyone but a French girl.

Brianna broke into her own thoughts with an impatient exclamation. Why on earth was she wasting time thinking about Philippe and his taste in girl-friends? She didn't care tuppence who he married or if he married at all. But she did think she might have been invited out to dinner tonight, that had really got her down. 'Be your age, Brianna,' she adjured herself. 'Don't have a fit of the sulks because you have to stay at home like Cinderella. Who knows, maybe the fairy godmother will turn up and you'll go to *some-body*'s ball.'

It didn't turn out exactly like that, but neither did she stay home all afternoon either.

Philippe and Marie-Claude drove off and Olympe, exhausted from a night disturbed by her itchy insect bites, was asleep and so too was Jean-Christian. Tante Agathe came downstairs from her nap to the garden, where Isabelle and Brianna were playing a not very exciting game of croquet on the lawn. She was sitting in the shade of the chestnut tree doing some crochet when suddenly she exclaimed, 'Zut! I quite forgot to ask Violette to bring me a rabbit from the farm tomorrow. I'd planned to have one for dinner, then all the to-do with Olympe drove it right out of my mind.'

Isabelle threw down her croquet mallet. 'Brianna and I can go to the farm for you, Tante Agathe. We'll tell Madame Dupont what you want. A fine big rabbit jointed —and no head. Is that right?'

'That's certainly what I want,' Tante Agathe agreed. 'But you know Philippe prefers you to keep away from the farm, Isabelle.'

'Oh, he wouldn't mind if I went with Brianna. We can cycle out—the exercise will do us good. I have so much energy—this game of croquet isn't helping much at all. I'm in danger of sending a ball through the window any minute, I can tell you ... What do you think, Brianna? You said you'd like to visit the farm.'

'Yes, I would,' Brianna agreed a little dubiously. But she thought it rather ridiculous all the same that Philippe should put such silly limitations on Isabelle's freedom. She didn't see why his restrictions should apply to her anyhow, and having been excluded from the dinner, she felt a quite frustrating need to do something. She turned to Tante Agathe and told her firmly, 'We'll order the rabbit for you, Tante Agathe. It would be a pity to have to alter your plans.' Tante Agathe frowned and pursed her lips, and Brianna thought perversely, looking her straight in the eye, 'If you tell me what I may or may not do, then you'll discover I'm not always as agreeable as I have been since I've been living under your marvellous nephew's roof!'

Perhaps Tante Agathe read the message, because she said with a slight shrug, 'Very well—if you go together. And there'll be no need under the circumstances to—discuss it with Philippe.'

Isabelle suppressed a giggle and linked her arm through Brianna's as they made their way to the garage where the bicycles—there were two—were kept. And a few minutes later they were cycling along the road that Isabelle had taken that morning.

'Do we go past Philippe's vineyards?' Brianna wanted to know.

'No, we turn off along a little country road in a minute or two,' Isabelle said gaily.

The country road was narrow and rutted. Little wild strawberries grew along the verges, there was a wheatfield with the scarlet of *coquelicots* in it, and yellow flowers. Brianna revelled in the country scents, the blue of the sky, the flight of swallows.

'People don't visit each other's houses much in France, do they, Isabelle?' she called out. 'I mean, they don't just— drop in.' She was fishing, of course, trying to get Isabelle to talk about the Moreaus and Madame Hubert-Benoise, and she felt a little ashamed of herself, but she was unable to help her curiosity. She wobbled along on her bicycle behind Isabelle, sure that she was going to fall off soon, and won- dering if she should get off and walk before she regretted it. Isabelle, intent too on the effort of balancing, didn't answer her for several seconds, and then she said astutely, 'You mean you want to know why you weren't invited to Les Charmes. I'll tell you why. It's because Madame Hubert- Benoise prefers to ignore you and me. She wants Philippe to ask Albertine Moreau to marry him, so she doesn't want anyone else around.'

'Oh, is that how it is?' Brianna exclaimed, as if the notion were entirely new to her. 'And do you think he will?'

Her sister laughed scornfully. 'No! He'll never marry Bertine. She's far too soft for a man like Philippe.' She suddenly abandoned her efforts to cycle as the ruts in the road became deeper, and leapt to the ground. Brianna did likewise. Ahead, she could see the farm buildings, as she and Isabelle walked along slowly, wheeling their bicycles, the late afternoon sun still shining hotly from above.

'Nobody seeing us,' Brianna thought, 'would dream we're sisters.' Isabelle was so vivid with her bright black eyes and slightly swarthy complexion, and her corn-coloured hair whose colour, it was true, received some assistance from the chemist. And Brianna herself was so understated in every way.

'What do you mean, too soft?' she asked after a moment, as Isabelle showed no signs of saying anything further.

'Oh, she has no character. It wouldn't be much fun to him to control her when she always says, Yes, Philippe, and No, Philippe, and never, never argues. Philippe would rather have someone who fought him a little, don't you think so?' She glanced sideways at Brianna, looking decidedly coquettish despite, or perhaps even because of, those short yellow pigtails.

Brianna shrugged without answering. In her experience, Philippe practically demanded arguments and fights. But whether he found resistance to his will attractive in a woman was another thing altogether. She hardly imagined *she* had charmed him by her opposition, and she was inclined to think it more likely that Albertine, with her Yes, Philippe and No, Philippe, would endear herself to him.

'Well, *don't* you think so?' Isabelle persisted, and Brianna said mildly,

'I have no idea really. I haven't thought about what qualities Philippe would admire in a girl.'

'Haven't you? Well, I have, and I'll tell you a secret, Brianna. There's another reason why Philippe will never marry Bertine. I happen to know there's another girl in his life. So you see——' She fluttered her long lashes, and smiled provocatively.

'Another girl?' Brianna was surprised. 'Who is she?'

'Oh, I'm not going to say. I've already told you it's a secret. Philippe would be furious if I told anyone—besides, he isn't really aware that I know. But it's quite true. And it's because of her he hasn't married...' Suddenly she sprang back on to her bicycle. 'Look, we can ride the rest of the way. Old Dupont's patched up this part of the road.'

Brianna too climbed back on her bicycle, and after a few minutes, during which time she reflected futilely on the 'secret' her sister had told her, they reached the farm. A great iron *portière* opened into the farmyard, and beside it was a little gate through which Brianna followed Isabelle on foot, after they had propped their bicycles against the wall.

'You know the Duponts are peasants,' Isabelle said in an undertone. 'I shan't introduce you, you understand.'

Brianna didn't really understand, but she didn't comment, as two dogs ran out to meet them and gambolled around their feet. They went through a big stone archway into a cobbled yard where some cows were waiting to be milked, and tranquilly munching hay. They were enormous creatures, some of them black and white, some reddish.

'The *marron* ones are from Normandy,' Isabelle said knowledgeably. 'The black and white are Landes cows. Violette told me so.'

Above the milking shed, pigeons and swallows had nested in the rafters, while in the big yard a few hens clucked around and a gosling suddenly appeared and raced around frantically, giving the impression that it had lost its way. The man in the milking shed called out something that Brianna couldn't understand, and Isabelle answered that they wanted to see Madame Dupont about a rabbit. The man—it was Monsieur Dupont—shouted again, louder this time, with the result that a short stocky woman in a black dress and dark stockings emerged from a building across the yard. She was followed a few seconds later by a dark-haired, dark-faced young man in working clothes—handsome, sensual-looking and bold. He stopped in the shadows and, hands low on his narrow hips, stood staring at the two girls.

Isabelle strolled across the yard, and Brianna followed more slowly, avoiding looking at the staring man, looking instead at the huge stores of hay, the row of rabbit skins drying on some racks, the two-storied hutch with long-eared grey and white rabbits upstairs, and pretty little kitten rabbits down below. Bred for the table, of course, she thought with a slight feeling of revulsion. Yet after all, it wasn't any different from breeding lambs or calves to be eaten.

She heard Isabelle order the rabbit from Madame Dupont, and tell her firmly, 'We don't want the head', and then the man from the milking shed came across the cobbles and asked Brianna in thick and scarcely intelligible French if she wanted to see the the the cows being milked. She replied that she would like that, and followed him back to the shed. He wore dark blue overalls and beret, and his face was ruddy and rough, and the fact that she spoke French seemed to please him. He asked her, '*Anglaise?*' and she said yes, she was English, and wondered why on earth Philippe should have any objection to Isabelle's coming here. Monsieur Dupont was polite and friendly in a pleasant way. He showed her with pride the placid cows and the milking machines, the great refrigerated aluminium vat that held the milk, the mixer that stopped the cream from separating. The yard outside was a mess, but in here everything was clean. Brianna gathered, after having to request him to repeat what he'd said a couple of times, that the milk was

collected from the farm daily and taken to the *laiterie* to be
used for butter, cream and cheese.

Presently she thanked him for showing her around and
went to look for her sister. Madame Dupont had gone inside again, but Isabelle was leaning against the wall of the
farmhouse talking to the handsome young peasant Brianna
had observed earlier. Now she was somehow shocked at
the way the man was looking at her sister. There was something in the tableau that stunned her mentally for a moment
—the pretty sixteen-year-old with her blonde plaits bobbing against her cheeks, and the husky sensual-looking
peasant, standing so close to her, hips jutting, listening with
an attentive smile on his face to whatever she was saying.

Brianna moved forward.

'Isabelle——'

'I'm coming. One moment.' She saw the flash of her sister's small white teeth as she smiled up at the man. He
said something and she nodded, and then ran across the
yard to Brianna.

'Who was that?' Brianna asked her as outside once more
they mounted their bicycles and started on the way home.

'Emile Dupont. 'E is Violette's brother. I 'ave known 'im
many years ago. I meet 'im when I am ill and Maman sends
me to the country. 'E is 'andsome, no?' said Isabelle in her
appealing but atrocious English.

'Is he? I didn't really notice,' said Brianna, forgetting the
truth in her feeling of unease.

'Oh, Brianna! What's the matter with you?' Isabelle
slipped back into her own tongue. 'You must have noticed!
He's just so sexy—I nearly die when he talks to me. I get
the loveliest feeling all through my body——'

So that was why Philippe didn't like Isabelle to go to the
Dupont farm, Brianna mused. It was because of Emile. But
surely no harm could come of it. It gave Isabelle a thrill and
that was all. And after all, a girl of sixteen can have roman-

tic—even erotic—daydreams over any handsome man at
all and come to no harm. It was all perfectly normal and
natural. All the same, she herself had been vaguely disturbed by the feeling she had experienced in seeing those
two confronting each other. Thank heaven, she told herself,
Tante Agathe had said there would be no need for Philippe
to know about the little excursion.

Yet for some reason Isabelle herself was not content to
let their visit to the farm be relegated to oblivion. The following evening as they all enjoyed their meal of *lapin au
chou,* she referred quite casually to the fact that they had
gone to Dupont's farm.

'It's an excellent rabbit, isn't it, Tante Agathe? So juicy
and full of flavour. You see, I told Madame Dupont exactly
what you wanted. Emile wanted to know why you didn't
require the head.' She rolled her eyes and spread her hands
and looked at Philippe saucily. 'Men don't understand—
Emile laughed at me when I told him.' As if oblivious of the
displeasure on her stepbrother's face, she then took another
mouthful of food and exclaimed while it was still in her
mouth, 'Oh, that Emile! *Oo là là!* So handsome! Eh,
Brianna?'

Philippe flashed Brianna a furious look from under his
brows.

'So you went to the farm, the two of you. Why, may I
ask?'

'Oh, Philippe, haven't I said why? Tante Agathe
wanted——'

Tante Agathe interrupted agitatedly before she could go
on. 'Unfortunately I forgot to order the rabbit from Violette, Philippe, so to save me a change of plans the girls
offered to ride out to the farm. There was no harm in it.
They went together. Of course I would never have allowed
Isabelle to go on her own.'

'I'm positive Isabelle wouldn't want to go on her own,'

Marie-Claude put in. 'I went there once with Louis. Oh, the smell of the farmyard! And the dirt under one's feet! It was frightful! And some boy—one of Dupont's sons, I daresay, he has a good many—stood and stared the whole time. I've never felt so uncomfortable. It's the last time I'll go out there, I promise you. I'd sooner go without meat for a week.' She glanced across at Brianna. 'Didn't you find it disagreeable, Brianna?'

Brianna smiled faintly. Her feelings were very mixed, but one thing was clear in her mind—she didn't want to appear to side with Philippe. Yet neither did she want to disagree flatly with Marie-Claude who obviously meant well, and was probably trying to draw attention from Isabelle, who had been a fool to blurt out the story. The French seemed to enjoy wrangling, however. Isabelle had remarked on that yesterday, though in a slightly different context. But now she refrained from expressing any opinion at all, and continued to eat her meal though she was beginning to lose her appetite. Not so the rest of the family. They continued to eat with gusto while they carried on with expressing their warring opinions.

Philippe put into words how little Brianna's thoughts on the subject mattered.

'Brianna's impressions are quite irrelevant—the English probably have different ideas from ours in any case. The point is, I've made it clear that Isabelle is not to go to the Dupont farm—either alone or with her English sister. Please remember that in future, Tante Agathe.' He turned his blue eyes on Isabelle. 'You'll stay right away from Emile Dupont. Is that plain? He's a peasant—and you're only a child.'

Isabelle leaned her forearms on the table and tossed back her blonde hair, worn loose tonight and shimmering in the lamplight. 'But I'm *not* a child, Philippe. I tell you Emile doesn't think so!'

'I can be sure of that,' Philippe snapped. 'But such an acquaintance is not *comme il faut*, and I won't have it, do you hear?'

'Yes, I hear.' Isabelle pouted prettily. 'But I don't understand.' She glanced at Brianna and decided to speak in English. 'Brianna is not so narrow in the mind. She is my sister and she does not think it wrong that I talk with Emile. 'E is no different from us. 'E is like you, Philippe, with two legs, two arms, a body. 'E is not only a farmer—'e works among the vines as you do.'

'Oh, *tais-toi*!' Philippe said sharply. 'You're talking rubbish.'

'But it's true!' Isabelle insisted through another mouthful of her dinner. 'He's going to take me mushrooming, anyhow.'

'You won't go,' said Philippe briefly.

'But if Brianna comes with me, then it will be all right.'

'I've already said no.' Philippe glanced round the table at his womenfolk. 'You understand what I've said, Tante Agathe?'

'*Oui. D'accord*, Philippe.'

'Marie-Claude?'

'Yes, Philippe.'

'Brianna?'

Brianna caught her lower lip between her teeth. The idead of going mushrooming with Isabelle and Emile had little appeal for her, but she objected on principle to being expected to say 'Yes, Philippe' as meekly as the other two women had done. She was not one of his admirers. So instead of acquiescing, she said lightly, 'I'm afraid I can't think what all the fuss is about. Mushrooming is surely pretty harmless. As for the Duponts, they seem perfectly respectable people to me. I enjoyed myself at the farm yesterday. Monsieur Dupont was kind enough to show me the milking machines and so on, and it was very interesting.'

She raised her eyes and looked at Philippe, her cheeks red. 'You can't expect me to see eye to eye with you about every little thing, Philippe. I'm not your sister—and I prefer to think for myself.'

Philippe looked back at her and she felt herself quail inwardly. She almost expected him to raise his arm, point to the door, and tell her to get out. But after studying her face for a few seconds, he merely said, 'I'll have my coffee in the study, Tante Agathe. Isabelle, I'll talk to you there in five minutes.'

Now it was Isabelle's turn to say 'Yes, Philippe', which she did with what sounded very like a giggle.

Philippe left the room, and Brianna wondered if the silence that ensued was disapproval. Then Isabelle remarked jauntily, 'Philippe goes too far sometimes. Brianna is right— she must think for herself. She isn't part of the family.'

'How true,' thought Brianna, her feelings more confused than ever. She was a little surprised that she wasn't the one Philippe wanted to see in his study, and not Isabelle. She wondered if she would have backed down and accepted that order.

Tante Agathe made coffee and Isabelle was dispatched to the study with two cups. As for Brianna, she was thankful later to help stack the dishes in the kitchen ready for Violette the next morning, and then to excuse herself and go upstairs to her room.

There she took off her shoes and changed out of the long patio dress she was wearing into a soft house gown, in muted shades of blue and lilac. She curled up in a chair with a book she had brought upstairs from the salon a day or so earlier—Colette's *Gigi*, which until now she had read only in English.

She opened the book, but she didn't read more than two or three pages. She was feeling too churned up as a result of the altercation over dinner. It occurred to her that the whole thing could have been avoided if only Isabelle had had the sense to hold her tongue. Instead she had quite deliberately let Philippe know she had disobeyed his wishes and gone to the Dupont farm. Now as a result everyone—with the exception of Marie-Claude—was in some sort of trouble. Brianna wondered what was going on in Philippe's study at this moment, if Isabelle were being brought to her knees. She was very young after all, and despite her defiance Brianna didn't doubt that a man of Philippe's strength of character could quickly make her repent if he wished to do so. She was beginning to think that the Gaze girls were troublemakers all round! Philippe's opinion of her as 'objectionable' must now be confirmed.

She sighed a little and had turned back to her book when someone rapped sharply on the door and Philippe said commandingly, 'Brianna, may I come in?'

Her heart began to thud. She'd thought she was to escape scot free, that for her there was to be no lecture, but she'd underestimated Philippe's determination. She uncurled her legs and ran her fingers nervously through her silky hair.

'Yes—I suppose so.'

The handle of the door turned and he came in and stood looking down at her. He had removed the tie he wore at dinner and the top three buttons of his wine-coloured shirt were undone, revealing a strip of darkly tanned skin. Soft fawn cotton trousers clung to his narrow hips, and his blue eyes were screwed up as he continued to scrutinise her for several seconds without saying anything. Brianna wondered whether he was deciding on his method of attack or if he was merely summing her up. He was certainly taking her in very thoroughly in the gown that clung softly to her figure, and ridiculously she wished she were not so thin—that she had a little more figure for it to cling to.

Perhaps, she thought uneasily, disturbed by his gaze and feeling the colour begin to creep into her cheeks, perhaps he expected her to stand up instead of leaning back in the armchair and staring back at him.

He moved and rested one hand on the top of the carved oak chest that stood against the wall. The other hand was on his hip and there was a graceful ease in every line of his figure.

'Just what was your idea in taking that child to the farm yesterday? I'm aware Tante Agathe had put you in the picture as to my wishes, but obviously you made it difficult for her to insist you should concur with them.'

Brianna looked back at him, wishing her heart would stop thumping. It was absurd to feel like a guilty girl. Certainly Tante Agathe had said Philippe 'preferred' Isabelle not to go to the farm, but that was all. And everyone knew what it meant when Philippe expressed a preference, so there would be no sense in making a point of it. Besides, she didn't want to involve Tante Agathe more than necessary, so she merely said reasonably, 'The *idea*, as you put it, was to order a rabbit. I thought you knew. The rabbit you ate tonight, and seemed to enjoy very much despite the rather stupid row about it.'

A spark of anger fired in his eyes, but he said evenly, 'I'd have eaten it with equal enjoyment tomorrow night—and without the extra garnishing of a row, as you call it, *belle-soeur*. Which is the whole point of the matter, for you were the one, weren't you, who wanted so badly to visit the farm? Frankly I'd have thought you a little mature in years to become so excited about such a project, by the way.'

So she was to blame, was she? Who had put that idea into his head? Tante Agathe to protect Isabelle? Or Isabelle to protect herself? Well, it didn't matter. She could stand shouldering the blame. Philippe's displeasure meant very little to Brianna Gaze, and for sure he wasn't going to report the feuding between himself and her to Maman!

'You can think what you choose,' she said indifferently.

'But if you imagine I merely wanted to annoy you, then you can think again. The fact is, your farms are very different from English farms, and I wanted to see.' She sat up straight, feeling somehow at a disadvantage to have him looking down at her. After a moment she stood up and wandered to the window to look outside. It was dark, and the stars were beginning to show in a deep purple sky.

'Well,' he said from behind her, 'as you've already pointed out, I have no jurisdiction over what *you* do, but I will *not* have Isabelle fraternising with Emile Dupont. He's a peasant——'

'A peasant?' She swung round to face him scornfully. 'So what? That's only a word. He's a human being—a person—just as Isabelle said. Surely you don't think it's—unseemly or whatever to say *bonjour* to a peasant. That would be totally absurd. Isabelle's not a child——'

'Emile doesn't confine himself to a tug of the forelock and a humble *bonjour*,' Philippe said dryly. 'And as far as I'm concerned, no matter how often you or Isabelle or anyone else at all insists it's otherwise, Isabelle *is* a child, and will remain a child until she leaves school.'

'Oh, really! You're hopelessly out of date! Do you think that sort of idea holds in Paris, for instance—where my sister goes to school? A girl of sixteen is far from being a child these days.'

He made an impatient exclamation. 'Say what you like, but to me a girl of sixteen who is part of my family is a child to be protected. And for reasons that are quite clear to me if not to you, Isabelle is to have nothing more to do with Emile Dupont. She is not even to go mushrooming with him. It won't stop at that.'

Brianna laughed mockingly. 'It could go a lot further than hunting for mushrooms without any harm being done. Besides, there is such a thing as platonic friendship, *beau-frère*. Why don't you start trying to believe in it?'

She stared at him and he stared back, then quite suddenly, without her having the slightest idea it was going to happen, she was in his arms.

'This is why,' he said, and began to kiss her without mercy.

When he stopped, he still held her savagely by the arms, and looked down into her burning face.

'You're a woman and I'm a man,' he said. 'Nothing you can say will alter that, or the fact that I'm aware of it. Something draws us together—and that's a fact of nature. You may resist the pull, and I may not. So long as we both resist, there are no consequences, there's no danger. But are you going to tell me that Emile Dupont, whose passions haven't been tempered to any great degree by either sensitivity or learning, is going to resist a girl as enticing as Isabelle? Or that Isabelle, so young and innocent and so eager for excitement—so obviously and painfully aware of her femininity—has either the will or the desire to refuse him? I know my Isabelle. You call her "sister", but she's my sister far more than she's yours, make no mistake about it, and I know her a hundred times better than you do ... So I say no mushrooming, and an end to the acquaintance. It would be a pity, wouldn't it, if I had to deny both her and myself the pleasure of her coming to Huchet altogether?'

Brianna stood listening, and struggling for composure. Hardly knowing what she was saying, she told him, 'You're being over-protective. If—if she's the kind of girl you say, won't she get into just as much trouble in Paris, when you're not there to pull the cotton wool down around her ears?' She felt her nerves quivering, and she longed to throw herself down on the bed, to hide herself in darkness. Philippe's kiss had bruised, shaken—wounded her, reached deep within her to some hidden part of her she hadn't known existed, and she felt strangely humiliated. In a way she was as innocent as Isabelle, and she felt Philippe had

somehow treated her unfairly, without regard to the rules—
to *any* rules. But because she was English and he was
French, she wasn't going to admit it or let him know it
mattered to her. It was utterly crazy in her view that he
could seize her, kiss her the way he had, and then continue
calmly to discuss Isabelle. But if he could do it, then so
could she. All the same, she wished quite frantically that
she were back in England where she understood men and
their feelings—men like Peter Arden, uncomplicated, sane.
Yet even to think of Peter now seemed somehow laughable,
and because she could think such a thing, she felt ashamed
of herself. She liked Peter—very much. Whereas what she
felt for this man, Philippe d'Hellier——

She turned her back on him and told him, 'Isabelle's *my*
sister, not yours. Besides, we're both females, so don't dare
to tell me you understand her better than I do. You *don't*!'
She stopped, because her voice had began to shake uncon-
trollably.

'Very well. But at least accept that I understand Emile
Dupont and his—sexual urges better than either of you do,'
he said cruelly.

She didn't answer and presently she heard the door
closed firmly—but not slammed—as he left the room. She
sank down on the bed, bewildered. What was it all about?
Philippe had come to accuse her of leading Isabelle into
danger, but it wasn't true, it simply wasn't. A visit to a
farm was so simple. But to Philippe it seemed that nothing
was simple, and she didn't understand him.

She discovered she was pressing the back of her hand to
her mouth, where his lips had scorched hers.

CHAPTER FIVE

STRANGELY enough, and contrary to Brianna's expectations, the whole affair of Emile, that had caused something of a family row, seemed to blow over, and no reference was made to it at all during the next few days. Brianna had expected *some* repercussions, since she had refused to be brought into line by Philippe, but both Tante Agathe and Marie-Claude behaved towards her exactly the same as they had before, and, in fact, so did Philippe. Still, she took great care not to be left alone in *his* company.

She ran into Richard Hazelwood one day when she had taken Olympe for a walk in the *poussette*, and was able to pay back the money she owed him. He apologised for the delay in asking her to Les Charmes. He'd been suffering from a cold, he said, and as well, Madame Hubert-Benoise was being rather hard to get on with. But he promised it would not be long before he was able to entertain her. Brianna hoped he was right. She could do with a friend outside the family, because she had very strong and decided feelings within herself of not belonging. In fact, she was seriously considering whether it wouldn't be sensible to return to England and come back to France later, when her mother was back in Paris.

She was in the midst of trying to make up her mind about this when she had a letter from Peter Arden.

'You know what my mother thinks you should do, Bri?' he wrote. 'Come home to us! And I must say I agree with her. You went to France specifically to see *your* mother, didn't you? And she just flitted off to Switzerland. So it's been a flop. I'm sorry she's not well, of course, and I don't want to sound too sceptical—but surely she could have kept you up to date or managed to spend a *few* days with you. Anyhow, why don't you come home? You can always go back later, if you still feel like it. You have a clear conscience now, you did make the effort. Anyhow, I miss you. You've no idea how much.'

It was perhaps that final sentence that made up Brianna's mind for her. She positively couldn't go back. If she did, Peter might take all sorts of things for granted that she didn't mean, and Mrs Arden would try pushing them into marriage—and where that sort of thing was concerned, she told herself, she wasn't nearly as amenable as the French. Meanwhile here, she supposed at the very least she could be helpful with the children. As well, she supposed she was on good enough—though slightly negative—terms with Marie-Claude, and she was getting to know Isabelle. She pushed the whole business of Emile right to the back of her mind. Philippe could surely discipline Isabelle in his own way, with or without her support.

She found she had to make an effort, though not with a great deal of success, not to think about Philippe too much. About the way he had kissed her—the hostility between them—the girls in his life: Bertine and that other mysterious girl Isabelle had talked about. She just didn't want to know about that, she told herself. But of course she did. What girl could help being curious—even though she disliked intensely the man in question?

She was thinking about Philippe, unwillingly yet helplessly, when she went for a walk alone one evening. She had had a bad headache that day, and noticing her white face and the strained look on her face, Tante Agathe had banished her from the living room where, the shutters closed against the heat, Olympe was pestering Brianna to tell her a story. Jean-Christian, who was getting teeth, was crying, and the two other girls had gone for a walk in the cool woods to gather flowers. Isabelle had asked Brianna to go with her, but she had refused, aware that her sister's ceaseless chatter wouldn't help her head.

'I have some letters to write, Isabelle.'

'Oh—to Peter Arden.' Isabelle had said knowingly, and Brianna hadn't contradicted her. At all events, Marie-Claude had gone with Isabelle instead.

Then half an hour later, Tante Agathe told her, 'You must get some fresh air, Brianna. It's plain you have a bad headache. I can manage the children. Go for a walk by the stream where it's cool and quiet. I'm sure your letters can wait.'

Brianna hadn't walked down to the stream before, and now she found it was a delightful place, cool and quiet just as Tante Agathe had said. Some of the women from the village had done their washing there and spread it to dry on the bushes, and in the shade of the leafy trees the little stream—the Huchet—plashed gently along.

Soon Brianna sat down in the long grasses and stared at the water, letting its soft music soothe her senses. Yet, annoyingly, it wasn't long before her brain was busily turning over all sorts of things about Philippe. Impatient with herself, she left the stream and began to walk back towards the village. She came to the conclusion that she needed to see other people to keep herself from becoming obsessed by her complicated and irritating feelings towards Philippe. To go back to England and Peter was certainly not the answer, but it might help if she could see more of Richard. If only that old grandmother of his would stop being so hard to get on with and let him invite her there, she was positive the tempo of her life would change for the better. She had half a mind, as she walked on towards the village, to storm Les Charmes—to ring the bell on that great old carved wooden door she had seen through the iron gates and ask if Richard Hazelwood was at home. This sort of behaviour might pass unremarked among the people she mixed with in Canterbury, for parents weren't dragons there and neither were grandmothers. But how would it go in Huchet-les-Anges? She had no idea. Quite possibly it might embarrass Marie-Claude or Philippe if it got back to their ears—and Philippe would say that the English had no manners.

Brianna reached the *place* and still hadn't made up her mind. The tables outside the Café des Vignes looked enticing in the shade of the big tree that grew there, and a little weakly she decided to have a glass of lemonade and reach a decision over it. To storm Les Charmes or not—that was the question.

She reached no conclusion at all, but she knew she was terribly tempted, and part of the temptation was the desire to have a glimpse of Albertine Moreau, who might or might not be there ...

'*Bonjour, ma petite belle-soeur.*' Philippe d'Hellier's voice broke in on her reverie. 'Are you waiting for anyone in particular, or may I join you?'

'Join me, by all means,' she said, aware her heart had started its thudding. 'How did you manage to find me here?' she added, as he pulled out a chair and sat down opposite her.

'Oh, I wasn't looking for you—it was pure chance,' he said dampeningly. 'I was driving home and happened to see you.' He turned to order himself an aperitif from the waiter who came hurrying out from the café bar, then tilted his brows at Brianna. 'Something for you?' She shook her head and after a moment he told her with a quizzical smile, 'I thought I'd seize the opportunity to have a quiet talk with you.'

'Really? What have I done to deserve that?'

'Come now, don't be so distrustful of me. I'm not going to give you a lecture,' he said, his expression hardening slightly. 'We surely have several common interests even if we sometimes disagree with each other ... You've been avoiding me deliberately since the night we disagreed about Isabelle's upbringing, haven't you?'

Brianna shrugged. 'Perhaps. But that's certainly something I don't intend to talk about. I've said all I have to say about that.'

'And so have I,' he agreed significantly as the waiter placed his aperitif before him. He turned sideways in his chair, crossing his long legs, and picking up his glass to look at Brianna over it. 'I had a letter from Switzerland today. My *belle-mère* is improving steadily and is anxious for news of us here in Huchet. I think she might be pleased if you'd write her a letter ... I hope everything's to your satisfaction—that you don't have any complaints?'

'What an extraordinary thing to suggest!' she said coolly. 'I didn't come here looking for faults.'

'I apologise,' he said at once, twisting his glass around abstractedly between finger and thumb. 'I've expressed myself badly. I'll try again. Let's see—Are you happy here with us?'

For an instant their eyes met and Brianna had a fleeting vision of his face as it was that night he had kissed her in her room, and she wondered if he even remembered it.

'Oh yes, I'm happy.' She spoke nervously, her glance falling. 'I'm happy on the whole, that is. Tante Agathe is always pleasant to me, which is good of her, seeing you did your best to show me up in a bad light over the incident of the farm, didn't you?'

A spark of surprise showed in the blue fire of his eyes as he exclaimed impatiently, 'Don't talk rubbish! You put yourself in a bad light. You're argumentative and hasty.'

'Thank you,' she said furiously. 'Another compliment from you. I'm overwhelmed!'

His eyebrows lifted. 'You don't agree you're argumentative?'

Brianna pressed her lips together. Perhaps she was lately, but not as a rule, not when she had reasonable people to deal with. But Philippe was so dogmatic and arrogant.

'Not unduly,' she said, and added, 'No more argumentative than you are, anyhow.'

He laughed briefly. 'Well, let's not argue about *that*, anyhow. But to continue with this matter of your rather moderate happiness. I hope you find Marie-Claude agreeable, as well as Tante Agathe?'

'Oh yes, they're all quite nice to me.'

'Excepting me?' he suggested. 'It's true I've taken no chances with you, but that's the result of first impressions——'

'You thought me an objectionable girl,' she said, colouring with annoyance. 'But are such impressions indelible? Couldn't I be allowed to make a fresh start after all this time?'

'You could—if you didn't continually rush in to the attack, thereby spoiling your chances.'

'You're exaggerating.' She leaned back in her chair a little wearily, glancing at her empty glass and rather wishing she had asked for another drink—something more potent than lemonade, preferably. She certainly needed something to help her swallow down such an unpalatable and large dose of Philippe d'Hellier's company! 'You provoke me. I have to defend myself.'

'Is that how you see our encounters? I'll have to cast my mind back. It may comfort you to know you have one champion in Huchet, however.'

'Isabelle?' she said at once.

'No, not Isabelle. Marie-Claude. She made a confession to me the other evening.'

'About what?' Brianna asked, puzzled.

'An apparently intense and bitter feud that existed between you two when you came over after our parents married. My sister says that looking back, she doesn't blame you at all for making yourself so unbearable you had to be shipped off back to England. She admitted to teasing you cruelly—about your accent, your clothes, your lack of taste and sophistication—every mortal thing she could think of. Is that true?'

Brianna coloured and shrugged. 'I suppose so. But girls at that age can be very intense. I'd prefer to forget it. I'm certainly not proud of the way I behaved, anyhow. I hadn't wanted to go to France, you see. I felt I belonged heart and soul to the English side of the family, and I was more or less expecting to be disliked. Besides, we were all under stress of some kind, with deaths and marriages and all the changes in the family groupings. You were right out of it, down here in the country.'

Philippe had listened to her thoughtfully, watching her face as she spoke, and now he said slowly, 'I wasn't as remote as you imagine. I was twenty-six, you know, a mature adult, and concerned that my father's remarriage should be a success. When I went up to Paris it was obvious that your presence wasn't helping matters. You had your mother so upset she was practically a nervous wreck, and as you were so plainly a fish in the wrong pond, I urged my father to send you back to England. It might have been a mistake. In time I daresay you'd have adjusted. I should have dragged you down here for a while—taught you to speak French, let Tante Agathe nurse you through your *crise*. And then how very different everything would have been! You'd have been a real little Parisienne by now.'

He smiled, but Brianna said perversely, 'I'm quite happy the way I am, thank you. Funnily enough, I like being English.' She didn't remark that her grandmother had appreciated her presence in England. 'But of course I'll write to Maman and tell her how much I'm enjoying staying at Huchet-les-Anges. I won't mention controversial matters.'

'And neither shall I,' he said sardonically. 'Please excuse me—I'll get some cigarettes and then if you're ready you can come home with me in the car.'

She watched him walk across the square, admiring absentmindedly his straight figure, the careless swing of his movements, the shine of his dark hair in the evening sunlight. Then, impatient with herself, she turned the other way. Across the square, she saw a woman emerge from the tiny P.T.T. She was a beautifully dressed, aristocratic-looking old lady with an arrogant and regal manner which suggested she was either one of the wealthy wine growers of the area, or perhaps a Parisienne who had bought a residence down here as a retreat. She made her way along the footpath with only a brief glance in Brianna's direction, and by the time Philippe returned, she had vanished into one of the narrow streets.

Brianna didn't discover that the woman she had seen was Madame Hubert-Benoise, until the following day. She discovered it then because quite unexpectedly she was at last invited to visit Les Charmes—an invitation passed on by Richard when she encountered him in the *boulangerie* during the morning.

'Oh, you're just the person I want to see, Brianna! Grand'mère's suddenly decided it's time you came to Les Charmes. Can you manage it this afternoon? That would suit me, if you can escape from those infants you've been mothering. Actually, I *was* supposed to drive over to Armette to fetch Bertine. Grand'mère has decreed that her beautiful grandchild is to take a holiday and spend at least two weeks at Les Charmes. But it appears your stepbrother's going to pick her up for some reason or other, which will probably gladden Bertine's heart because——' He broke off and exclaimed with a laugh, 'My God, I'm becoming a gossip since I came to Huchet! Well, not to worry—I'll discontinue the stream of consciousness or unconsciousness or whatever it is and return to the point. Which is, how about it, this afternoon?'

'This afternoon will be fine,' Brianna said gaily. She had been dying to go to the manor house, and she had had the feeling that Madame Hubert-Benoise's failure to approve it was a definite snub. She had met Louis briefly once when he brought Marie-Claude home after they'd been out together, and found him older than she had expected—close to Philippe's age, at a guess. Which had made her conclude that Bertine would be well into her twenties—suitably mature for Philippe, even if she was docile. Perhaps she would meet Bertine today, and she found that she both wanted it and didn't want it. At any rate, if Philippe was fetching her from Armette, it seemed to indicate that he had rather more interest in her than Isabelle claimed was likely.

After parting from Richard she hurried home, ready to announce her plans so that arrangements could be made as to who was to help Tante Agathe with the children during the afternoon. Marie-Claude was dressed ready to go out, and explained rapidly that she had suddenly discovered she had an appointment with the hairdresser in Dijon—an arrangement made a month ago.

'Would you like to come with me, Brianna?' she asked.

'I *would* have liked it,' Brianna said, slightly disappointed. 'But I've just been asked to go to Les Charmes this afternoon—by Richard Hazelwood.'

Marie-Claude caught her lower lip between her teeth and a curious expression crossed her face and disappeared again. 'Oh, then you must go, of course. You'll enjoy that far more than a day in Dijon. I suppose you have much in common with Richard since you're both English,' she added with a smile that seemed strained.

'We're both half English and half French,' Brianna said lightly. She had the feeling that her inability to go to Dijon had somewhat hurt her stepsister's feelings, which was quite absurd.

Isabelle made a fuss when she was told the news.

'Now I suppose Tante Agathe will expect me to hang around and hand-feed Micheline's children—and I'm not even their real aunt! I'm beginning to wonder why I came here for this vacation.'

'You could have gone to Honorine in Nice,' Tante Agathe reminded her placidly.

'No, I couldn't. Brianna was coming, and Philippe wanted me here. And now she's made this English friend and she's going to spend all her time going out with him——'

'Oh, *Isabelle*!' Brianna felt suddenly impatient with her. 'Don't be so ridiculous! It's just one afternoon!'

'Well, you shouldn't be going out with him at all,' Isabelle grumbled. 'You've already got a boy-friend in England. Anyhow, I'm not going to stay home. I shall cycle out to Les Fleurons and make a nuisance of myself to Philippe,' she added, tossing her hair.

'You won't be able to do that, *ma chère*,' said Tante Agathe tartly. 'Philippe won't be there—he's going to Armette today. There's a meeting of the syndicate, and then I understand he's going to collect Albertine Moreau, who's coming to stay with her grandmother for fifteen days.'

'That Madame Hubert-Benoise!' Isabelle exclaimed furiously. 'She orders everyone about . . . Then I'll go to Dijon. Wait for me, Marie-Claude, while I change my clothes.'

Marie-Claude sighed as Isabelle flew into the house from the garden where they had been talking. 'What a child! I'm afraid she's been spoiled.' She smiled at Brianna apologetically. 'Forgive me for saying so, Brianna, but the youngest one is always spoiled—I know, because I was the youngest of the family for a long time.'

Brianna said reluctantly that perhaps she would stay home after all, but Tante Agathe wouldn't hear of it.

'The children are no worry. Olympe is a good little girl, and as for the baby—he's no trouble since he hasn't yet reached the crawling stage. Philippe worries about me too much. You can all go out and enjoy yourselves today. That will be a rest for me.'

So at about three o'clock that afternoon, Brianna went— though whether she entirely enjoyed herself was another matter.

Les Charmes was certainly an impressive old place. Inside, beyond the great iron gates, was a huge garden bright with roses and hydrangeas, trailing wistaria, tubs of petunias and geraniums, the latter in every shade of red and pink. There were even some tall blossomy hollyhocks of a lovely pale yellow that reminded Brianna intensely of England. A caramel-coloured spaniel, belonging to Louis, came in a dignified way to meet her as she crossed the garden with Richard, who had been on the look-out for her.

As they went inside the house she looked about her with interest, and Richard told her, 'There's a vaulted cellar underneath, with an underground passage to the church, of all things. It's blocked up now, but was used centuries ago in the days of religious troubles, so Grand'mère says. Maybe I'll take you down there later, if you're interested, but first of all you have to see the old girl.'

She went up a graceful stone stairway with Richard to a huge high-ceilinged room furnished with elegant antique furniture. There, Madame Hubert-Benoise was sitting on a brocaded chaise-longue, and Brianna recognised her instantly and with a slight shock as the woman she had seen in the *place* the previous day. It was on the tip of her tongue to exclaim, 'I saw you yesterday!' but she refrained. She wondered, however, if the old lady had seen her and Philippe sitting together at the table on the pavement. She surely must have, for the square had been practically deserted.

'So you're the d'Helliers' English relation,' Madame Hubert-Benoise remarked when Richard had introduced them with scrupulous formality. 'Do you speak French, *mademoiselle*?'

'*Oui, madame*,' Brianna replied, feeling unaccountably nervous. '*Un peu.*'

'A little! It's to be hoped you're being modest, for I want to talk to you. Sit down. We must become acquainted. Richard, go away and occupy yourself with something else while this girl and I have a talk.'

Richard raised his eyebrows wryly. 'I'd rather sit here quietly and listen, Grand'mère. What are you going to tell Brianna? I'd like to make sure you're not going to warn her against me. I've already told her I'm, at the moment, a penniless artist.'

'*Oh là!* as if I'd bother! You're both English, it's a suitable enough friendship,' Madame Hubert-Benoise said dismissively, and Brianna thought, 'Oh dear, she doesn't like the English.' She had the feeling that this domineering old lady would have little trouble in arranging matches, and was quite ready to concede that the manor house could have its attractions for Philippe, who doubtless had the money to spend on repairs quite evidently needed. The walls in Philippe's home were a combination of plaster and rough stone, both very attractive. Here, the ancient plaster was crumbling away, and the ancient and once beautiful stone flooring was in obvious need of attention. The tapestry seat covers were fraying as were the floor rugs, and the long curtains at the enormous windows looked as if they were held together by the dust of ages.

But Madame Hubert-Benoise herself was beautifully and expensively gowned, and she wore diamonds on her fingers and an emerald brooch at the lacy throat of her dress.

'Now let's hear something about you, *mademoiselle*,' she said after Richard had disappeared, threatening that he would be back in fifteen minutes and if he wasn't allowed in then would set fire to the house—all of which was listened to with slightly amused indulgence by his grandmother. 'What's your connection with the d'Hellier family? Louis wasn't clear about it ... You've met my grandson, Louis Moreau?'

'Yes, *madame*. I'm not related to the d'Helliers at all, actually.'

'No? Then come, come—explain yourself.'

'I'm Isabelle's sister. You must know her.'

The old lady tilted her head arrogantly. 'Can it be possible? I'd already discarded that thought. You're plainly English, while Isabelle is French. Ah, that child! She's so spoilt! She runs wild ... Perhaps you mean you are her half-sister?'

'No, *madame*, we share the same parents. Our mother is now married to Monsieur d'Hellier, as you know. Our father was English, and I was brought up in England, by my grandmother, after my father died. But my grandmother died recently——'

'And you've come to France to help yourself to the d'Hellier name?'

Brianna blinked. 'I beg your pardon?'

Madame Hubert-Benoise didn't repeat her remark but asked instead, 'Is it strong family feelings that have brought you to France? Or have you been left with nothing?'

'I've been left well provided for,' said Brianna, beginning to feel more than a little irritated by all these questions. 'In England,' she reflected, 'we're a little more tactful and reticent in asking about financial matters,' but here they were discussed straightforwardly and without apologies, in a very businesslike way. 'My father left me property,' she continued, deciding to give good measure after all, 'and my grandmother left me money. I have no financial worries at all, *madame*.' She finished silently, 'Does that answer your question?'

'Then you've come for a visit only.'

'Yes. Mainly to see my mother.'

'So? But your mother is in Switzerland ... Well, I don't suppose you'll want to stay for long. French and English don't mix well. They never have and they never will. They've never really learned to like each other. Individually, one makes the effort again and again, but it's a case of being unable to communicate on any level that really matters. I understand these things. My daughter Pascale married an Englishman—Richard's father. We couldn't bear each other, he and I.'

'But *she* could *bear* him,' Brianna said dryly, and then was appalled at herself. What on earth had made her say such a tactless thing?—she who understood very well from her own experience what Madame Hubert-Benoise was talking about. Meanwhile, Madame was really glaring at her.

'I can't accustom myself to girls who are rude to their elders.'

'I'm—sorry, *madame*,' Brianna said quietly.

The other woman didn't return to the subject of her daughter's marriage. Instead, she pronounced, 'One finds it hard to believe you have any French blood in your veins. Your appearance, your manner, both are entirely English.' Brianna had an impulse to say 'Thank you' to that, but she refrained. 'You're like your father, one must assume?'

'Yes.' She moved restlessly. She wasn't enjoying one little bit sitting here being dissected in this curious and unmethodical way, what's more, as if she were a scorpion rather than a harmless beetle, she thought, to amuse herself. She was positive already that Madame Hubert-Benoise didn't like her, and was probably revising her opinion that her friendship with Richard was acceptable. Exactly what was the object of this private conversation? she wondered. She glanced surreptitiously at the little gilt clock that stood on a graceful chest, to check how much longer it would be before Richard would come to her rescue. Oh, heavens, how slowly the time was going. And in here in this subdued light, with the shutters half closed, she suddenly felt almost stifled, and the expensive perfume that Madame Hubert-Benoise wore drifted to her nostrils with nauseating sweetness.

'Well, now we know where we are,' Madame Hubert-Benoise said unexpectedly, 'I have no objections to your seeing something of Richard.'

'Thank you, *madame*.' She added beneath her breath, 'I didn't realise it required your permission.'

'I like to know with whom the members of my family are mixing. I don't approve of an indiscriminate mixing of young people, regardless of background and family. Marriages, in my opinion, are best not left to chance—and marriages hinge upon acquaintance.'

Brianna uttered a little laugh. '*Madame*, I hope you don't imagine that Richard and I——'

'I imagine nothing about my grandson and you. I don't pretend to understand the English. I simply see it as my duty to meet any girl who interests herself in Richard.'

'I haven't—interested myself in Richard,' Brianna protested with some heat, not liking the implications of that statement. Madame Hubert-Benoise turned hard eyes on her, her mouth curving in a cynical smile.

'Oh, you are interested! Of course you are. You're young, attractive, unmarried, and Richard is a good-looking young man. On a holiday one naturally looks for diversion of some kind with members of the opposite sex. It has always been so, even when I was a girl. Don't think because I'm half a century older than you that I don't know anything about being young and being interested in men. I know—I haven't forgotten.' Now she too glanced at the clock, and leaned forward, her bright eyes fixed intently on Brianna. 'I shan't interfere if you and Richard amuse one another—the English go their own way. With my French grandchildren—with Louis and Albertine Moreau—I am naturally more concerned. You know, undoubtedly, that Marie-Claude and Louis are expected to announce their engagement very soon?'

'I've heard rumours of it,' Brianna agreed, wondering what this was all leading up to.

'Do you know also that we expect Philippe and Albertine to marry?'

Brianna blinked as though she had been flicked on a raw place. 'No,' she said steadily. 'I've heard—nothing about that.'

'No?' The smile she gave showed plainly she didn't believe Brianna's denial, and had noticed her reaction. 'Then believe me when I say such a union is planned.'

'By whom?' Brianna longed to ask, but she didn't dare, not with those steely eyes regarding her so relentlessly. She could feel her pulses beating and was disturbed that she should be so positively knocked off balance. She had no idea whether or not Philippe wanted to marry Albertine Moreau. He had told her once that he was not married, not engaged, and had no mistress, but that meant nothing. Nor did Isabelle's opinion that he would never marry the Moreau girl count for anything. There was, however, the matter of that 'other girl' about whom Isabelle professed to know, and it suddenly occurred to Brianna that the other girl could well be a married woman, in which case he might well decide to marry Albertine.

'You appear sceptical, *mademoiselle*. But you must remember we have logical minds in France. We love—ah yes, we are great lovers!—but at the same time we are aware of the foolishness of leaving marriage to chance. And most fortunately we have discovered that love, which common sense tells us is mostly the result of proximity, can be cultivated, if sound plants from good stock are put in the ground at the right time ... Just so do we, in Huchet-les-Anges, cultivate our vines.'

Brianna this time tried to keep her face expressionless so as not to be accused of scepticism again. But sceptical she was, because if Madame was referring obliquely to Philippe and Albertine—surely this idea of cultivating love between them was a little late in the day, seeing that Philippe at least was well over thirty!

'With the vine,' Madame Hubert-Benoise resumed thoughtfully, 'we are at the mercy of nature—of frost, of hail, of beating rain or a high wind in summer. Our harvest can be ruined overnight. But in the case of *l'amour* most fortunately we can avert catastrophe by vigilance ... And with love as with the vine there are three crucial stages when we must be especially watchful. At the time when the young shoots sprout, again when the flowers are put forth, and finally when the grapes are ripe and one must judge to a hair's breadth the exact time to begin the harvest.'

She broke off, linking her fingers together and looking down at them for a moment, at her diamond rings sparkling in a shaft of sunlight that came through the half-closed shutters. Then she raised her head and smiled to herself, evidently enjoying her little allegory.

'So with the love that is being nurtured between Philippe and Albertine. The shoots have sprouted, yes. There have been blossoms in abundance. Soon now it will be time for the harvest. Do you understand the importance of what I am saying—of the critical stage we have now reached? Unfortunately, like Richard, you are English, your palate is both insensitive and uneducated not only to the taste of fine wines but also to the understanding of what family unions mean to us in France. But do not, I warn you, walk clumsily about this vineyard, trampling down vines that have been cultivated with such tenderness.' She paused again and Brianna thought, 'What on earth is she talking about? What does she think I've been up to?'

'I'm sorry, *madame*,' she said bewilderedly, 'I'm afraid I don't know what you mean.'

'No? I think you know very well, *mademoiselle*.' The words were almost hissed out. 'You were enjoying yourself yesterday with Philippe in the *place*, were you not?'

'In the *place*?' Brianna echoed in amazement, and suddenly realised that Madame Hubert-Benoise suspected her of having designs on Philippe. That was really laughable! But for heaven's sake—simply because she had shared a café table with him—— It was too ridiculous altogether. She felt a quite hysterical desire to laugh.

'Do you think, *madame*, that my presence might be—disturbing to Philippe?'

An expression of intense annoyance crossed the haughty old face. 'I think no such thing,' Madame Hubert-Benoise snapped. 'But I think you may very well have it in mind to disturb him. You are a pretty girl, yes, but nevertheless you are not in the least to his taste—so English, so lacking in sublety and sensitivity.'

Brianna grimaced and bit her lip. What an opinion this woman had formed of her in a quarter of an hour, and how unpleasant it was to be informed of it! And here was she, imagining she had acquired quite something in the way of poise ...

'No, you are not to be feared. You are no more than a little grey cloud that comes into the blue sky threatening rain—and will finally blow away on the wind ... But I do not like little clouds in my sky, and I speak plainly to you out of consideration for my little Bertine, who is so sensitive, so easily hurt. Yes, for that reason only. Stay away from Philippe, *mademoiselle*. Don't try to insinuate yourself into his life—don't meddle.'

Brianna stared at her speechlessly. So this was the object of the conversation! She was actually being warned to leave Philippe alone, and not very politely either. It was a relief to hear Richard knock once at the door, then to have him come into the room and ask lightly, 'Is the talk over? And has it left my reputation unsmirched?'

'Completely.' Brianna answered both questions at once, smiling and getting to her feet. She had wanted to meet Richard's grandmother, now she didn't particularly care if she never saw her again. 'There are Frenchwomen and Frenchwomen,' she thought. Tante Agathe was a sweetie, but Madame Hubert-Benoise was not her cup of tea at all. To think she had seen her sharing a drink with Philippe in the *place* and had apparently decided on the spot that she was trying to seduce him, or something equally ludicrous. So she had snapped her fingers, Richard had issued an invitation, and—hey presto! she had Brianna Gaze on the mat, being cut down to size. Not again, Brianna told herself. She didn't take kindly to being told not to meddle when she didn't want to meddle in any case. How she wished she could meet Albertine now, and see for herself what this so sensitive, so easily bruised plant was like!

As she left the room with Richard after saying a very polite goodbye to his grandmother, she tried to conjure up a picture of 'my little Bertine', and there came into her mind the image of a young woman approaching thirty, timid, obedient, murmuring 'Yes, Philippe' and 'No, Philippe' and shrinking frightened into her shell if he so much as looked at another woman. A hopeless sort of wife for Philippe, she told herself.

Richard hurried her downstairs and took her through a dim passage to a sunny room at the side of the house, with windows looking onto the garden. It was furnished with a

long work bench, some open shelves, a couple of stools and
very little else.

'My studio,' he told Brianna proudly. He had arranged
five or six oil paintings against the wall and he indicated
them with a slightly nervous wave of his hand. She stood
back and looked at them—soft colours speaking of a country summer, the green of vines, the blue of sky, the silver-
grey of a church steeple. Again—the dark blur of a forest on
a hillside, trees that looked as though a high wind were
passing through them. Birds being blown across the sky,
poppy petals floating across a wheatfield. Lastly, a ragged
sunflower lifting an indomitable face to a sun that was a
sunflower too.

They were poetic paintings, and she was surprised because in so many ways Richard Hazelwood appeared to be
a very ordinary young man. She wondered, after all, that
Madame had offered her Richard, even though they were
both English.

'I don't know what to say,' she said after a moment of
looking at him seriously. 'I'm not pretending they're great,
or anything like that, but I'm sure you have tremendous
talent. That sunflower—it's sheer poetry—it makes me
want to cry. Do you know Blake's poem, "Ah, Sunflower,
weary of time"? It reminds me of that for some reason.'

'You're the most rewarding viewer I've had,' he said
with a grin. 'I'll have to employ you to do some P.R. work
for me with my father ... Of course, frames will make a
difference—and cost a packet too. I'll make you a present
of *Sunflower*—I can get it framed in Armette for you.'

'That's too generous of you, Richard,' she said. 'Couldn't
I——'

'*No*,' he said flatly, anticipating that she was going to
offer to pay for the painting. 'What was Grand'mère talking to you about? Not me, I hope! I sometimes think she'd
like to straighten me out—get me married to a nice steady

girl and settled back in a nice steady job—preferably in England.'

'Oh, she wasn't talking about you,' Brianna said after a second. 'Just about my—my relationship to the d'Helliers, and she wanted to know why I'd come to France—that sort of thing. And then,' she added with a smile, 'she was telling me about growing grapes.'

'Growing grapes? Good lord! I hope you were interested. She's an extraordinary old girl, isn't she?'

'Extraordinary,' Brianna agreed.

They were in the garden drinking orange juice some time later when a motor came up the drive and stopped at the side entrance. Brianna recognised the car as Philippe's and despite herself her heartbeats quickened. So she was to meet Albertine after all, and satisfy her curiosity! Though somehow she knew it was more than mere curiosity that made her want to see this girl whose name was linked with that of Philippe d'Hellier.

CHAPTER SIX

ALBERTINE was small and dark-haired and pretty, and very young-looking. In fact, she looked no older than Isabelle, though Brianna learned later that she was actually nineteen. Her appearance took Brianna so completely by surprise that the English girl hardly heard Philippe, who had come with her from the car, making the introductions.

Bertine smiled at her guardedly and murmured that she had heard all about Brianna from Philippe, and Brianna replied that she too had heard about Bertine from Philippe, which was completely untrue. The thing was, one had only to look at this child to want to protect her, and those words of Madame Hubert-Benoise's—'My little Bertine is so easily hurt'—suddenly had a very real meaning. Brianna caught Philippe's eye on her, cold, calculating and cynical, and she thought so vehemently that she almost felt she must have said the words aloud, 'You beast! To let this gentle little girl have such hopes when all the time there's someone else.'

Well, *she* wasn't going to hurt Bertine, and when the girl asked her if she would come into the house with her, she said robustly, 'No, thank you—I was just about to leave. Tante Agathe will be expecting me to help with the children.' Ignoring Philippe—leaving him all to Bertine—she turned to Richard. 'I must go now—really!' She raised her face to his deliberately inviting him to kiss her which he did without hesitation. Bertine would see *she* had no interest in trying to entice Philippe away! 'It's been a lovely afternoon,' she told him. 'And you know what I said just now—in the studio? I really meant it!'

'You mean——' he began, and she interrupted with a smile,

'Oh, you know what I mean, *chéri*.' She linked her arm through his and said a final goodbye, then began to walk towards the gate.

'What *were* you talking about?' Richard asked her, sounding puzzled. 'And what's the sudden hurry?'

'I was talking about what I thought of your work, of course—that's all. And I'm in a hurry because—oh, because Bertine will have to go and see your grandmother and I'm sorry, Richard, I know she's a character and a fantastic old lady, but I've had my audience with her and I don't want to join the party and be too late home. I'm a little bit worried about leaving Tante Agathe to herself. Marie-Claude and Isabelle will probably be late getting back from Dijon, so I really should make tracks ... I'd like to go with you to Armette when you see about having that painting framed, though—and I wish you'd at least let me pay for the framing.'

'No fear—you're a friend,' he said emphatically.

'Then don't show your appreciation of your friends in that way too often,' she advised him ruefully, 'or you'll never make a living as an artist. Just think what these paintings may be worth one day when you're really famous!'

'You think I will be?'

'Of course!'

'You wonderful girl!' He swung her round suddenly and hugged her, kissing her enthusiastically right at the gate, and over his shoulder she saw Philippe's car glide to a slow halt, only a few feet away.

Philippe put his head out of the window. 'You'd better come home in the car with me, Brianna, since you're so worried about Tante Agathe,' he said in a voice that was far from friendly.

Brianna's cheeks were red. 'I hope I haven't done something frightful to the family honour allowing myself to be kissed almost in a public thoroughfare,' she whispered to Richard.

'You'll live through it,' he grinned back at her as he opened the car door and helped her in.

Her lightheartedness dropped from her after fifteen seconds in the car with Philippe. All that kissing had been silly, but just the same he didn't have to look so grim about it all.

'Why are you looking so fierce?' she asked him eventually, after glancing once again at his set profile. 'Have I done something frightful? Or are you being disagreeable because you've had to leave Bertine? I didn't want you to, I assure you. I intended to walk home.'

He ignored that, and then rather sharply pulled on the steering wheel and turned the car into a side lane instead of following the road through the village. In a couple of moments they were bumping along an uneven track by the stream.

'Where are we going?' she asked, knowing she sounded aggressive but irritated by the fact that he hadn't taken any notice of her. 'Tante Agathe will be expecting me——'

'Then Tante Agathe will have to wait.' He pulled up in the shade of a great tree and turned to face her, his eyes intent. 'Are you having an affair with Richard Hazelwood?' he asked abruptly.

Brianna blinked twice, then widened her eyes. 'No!' she exclaimed, feeling the bright colour flood her cheeks.

'No? I got a different impression ... I had no idea either that you were in the habit of visiting him at Les Charmes.'

She hunched her shoulders casually. 'Am I expected to give an account to you of every move I make?'

'Don't be so provocative!'

'I'm sorry, I didn't mean to be provocative, I thought I was being realistic. You're always making mountains out of molehills, aren't you?' She moved uneasily under the regard of his angry eyes and added nervously, 'I'm not in the habit of visiting Richard at Les Charmes, actually. Today I was—summoned by Madame Hubert-Benoise——'

'Summoned?'

'Isn't that the right word? Perhaps I should try to put it into French——'

'What did she want?' he interrupted without ceremony.

She sighed. 'Oh, to meet me—to tell me that marriages don't happen haphazardly in the best families in France—something like that. She's a great old matchmaker, isn't she?'

'Most women are matchmakers,' he said briefly. 'And does she approve or doesn't she?'

'What on earth are you talking about?'

'About you and young Hazelwood of course. Isn't that what *she* was talking about—however obliquely? I don't pretend to be in the picture, but if you two have been behaving the way you were this evening, then it's no wonder if Madame H. B. thought it time for a few pertinent words.'

'Really! What I do is no business of hers,' Brianna retorted. 'But you French constantly amaze me. Richard and I happen to like each other, that's all.'

His brows tilted. 'Is that the way you keep your conscience quiet? You have someone hankering after you in England, haven't you? In another minute you'll be coming out with your little rigmarole about platonic friendships, but you're fooling yourself if you think you can stir up our friend Richard the way you did and keep the affair on a strictly platonic footing. He has a French mother, you know.'

'What do you mean, stir him up?' she asked angrily.

'Oh—hanging on his arm, whispering in his ear, talking mysteries. *Looking* at him as you did——'

She widened her eyes. 'Honestly! *Looking* at him! You're just incredible——'

'You're the one who's incredible, *ma chère*. A girl's eyes can incite a man to do anything. They're the most formidable weapon a woman can have, and you have singularly beautiful eyes, *mon ange*. You can't be so lacking in sophistication that you don't know their power—I've remarked on it myself before this.'

Her colour slowly deepened as they stared at each other. *His* eyes—what were they doing to her as they delved into her own like that? A tremor ran through her body and she caught her breath as his arms reached out to take hold of her roughly and pull her towards him. She felt the slithery silk of his sage-green shirt against her cheek before he jerked her face up to his and set his lips against her mouth in a kiss that spread flames through every particle of her being.

How could a man kiss with such instant passion? she wondered headily as his lips did things to hers that she had never experienced before. Out of nothing—out of the air— there was suddenly this thing leaping between them. Philippe kissed her roughly, mindlessly, thoroughly, as if he couldn't help himself, as if he were carried away completely. And the awful thing was that she was rapidly being carried away too. She just didn't want him to stop——

With a sharp movement she struggled against him and pulled herself free, to retreat shaken and with burning cheeks to her own side of the car seat.

'Kissing in cars!' he exclaimed after a moment, his voice uneven. 'It's not my scene at all. You bring out the very worst in me, Brianna Gaze.' He pulled a folded handkerchief from his trouser pocket and wiped his mouth on it.

'My lipstick,' she thought. It hadn't been disturbed by Richard's kiss—not in the least.

Philippe started up the car and said as he stepped on the

accelerator, 'In my life, *belle-soeur*, there's no such thing as a platonic friendship.'

'"There is in mine,' she said huskily. Her mind was in a tumult as well as her body. 'But not for you—not even that —I don't feel *any* kind of friendship for you.'

She saw his eyes glint mockingly as he turned his head in her direction. 'Don't go on—leave it there. You'll really trip yourself up in a minute, *chérie* ... Perhaps you'd better try to think of me as a brother,' he added ironically. 'My step-mother would like us all to become one big happy family. What do you think?'

Brianna made no reply. She knew she could never in a million years think of him as a brother, never do anything but dislike him. She stole a glance at him—at that hand-some, aloof profile—and she felt a troubled stirring within herself. Why on earth had he kissed her? Merely to prove to her that there was no such thing as a platonic friendship between a man and a woman—if the man chose for it to be otherwise? What did he *really* feel for Brianna Gaze? She drew a shallow breath. One thing was for sure—he didn't look on her as a sister——

She tore her thoughts away from the unprofitable line they were following to ask him brightly, 'How did the meeting go?'

'The meeting?' he repeated, sounding so completely lost that she wondered where his own thoughts had been.

'In Armette,' she persisted. 'I thought it was the meeting of some group of *vignerons*.'

'Oh, that. Everything proceeded with its usual precision. I shan't bore you with details that would be meaningless to you.'

So she was slighted. She didn't attempt to make con-versation after that.

At the house, Isabelle and Marie-Claude were back from Dijon after all, and while Marie-Claude prepared Olympe's supper, Isabelle sat in the living room reluctantly giving Jean-Christian his bottle. Brianna found Tante Agathe in the kitchen and offered to help, but was told that everything was under control. Philippe, instead of disappearing to his study as she had hoped he would, was sprawling, inelegantly for him, on the *canapé* in the living room, watching Isabelle feed the baby. Brianna hesitated in the doorway between kitchen and living room, feeling somewhat at a loss. Philippe seemed quite preoccupied and unaware of her, and she studied him through the screen of her lashes. He had loosened the bronze-brown and ivory tie he wore and undone the top buttons of his green shirt. His dark hair fell across his forehead, softening the lines of his face, and his mouth was relaxed. He looked somehow strangely tender as he watched the sixteen-year-old girl and the baby, drowsily sucking away at the teat of the bottle. Brianna, looking at him, felt a sharp pang in the region of her breast.

Isabelle raised her black eyes to his face and smiled, then turned towards Brianna.

'There's a letter for you upstairs in your room, Brianna. A great big fat one, from your boy-friend in England. Does he write thrilling love letters? That's the second in three days. I suppose he wants you back in his arms—perhaps if you stay away too long he'll come to France to fetch you——'

'Be quiet, Isabelle,' Philippe broke in sharply. 'Can't you grow up and learn to be discreet instead of babbling about other people's private affairs in that childish way? I'm really beginning to lose patience with you!'

'Oh!' Isabelle jumped to her feet, her face set and angry. 'Why are you always picking at me, ever since Brianna came? I can't do a thing right!' She thrust Jean-Christian, who had begun to howl loudly as the bottle was suddenly snatched from his mouth, roughly into Brianna's arms.

'Here, you take him, I'm—I'm——' She rushed from the room, her eyes bright with tears.

Brianna looked at Philippe accusingly. 'You didn't have to hurt her feelings by speaking to her like that. She didn't say anything that bothered me. You had the poor child in tears.' She stood glaring at him over the baby's head, and he stared back, his eyes hard.

'Isabelle can make the tears flow at will—she likes a scene. As for her being a poor *child*—aren't you always telling me she's not that? But child or not, it's time she learnt some manners, in my view, instead of blurting out details of other people's private lives.'

'There's nothing private about my receiving letters from Peter Arden,' she retorted. 'You seem to imagine you know all about him, anyhow.'

'I know rather more about Richard Hazelwood,' he said.

She pressed her lips together and said no more; she didn't want the conversation to develop into a wrangle about herself. But for Jean-Christian, whom she had been soothing automatically, she too would have left the room. As it was, she took the chair Isabelle had left so precipitately and let the infant continue feeding.

'There there, *mon p'tit coco*,' she murmured comfortingly, just as she had heard Tante Agathe say. She heard Philippe utter a sound very like a laugh, but she refused to look at him, and in a moment he got up and walked away. As he reached the door, she said levelly, 'I hope you're going to apologise to Isabelle.'

'I'm afraid your hopes are vain. She can recover from her fit of temper without my assistance.'

'Beast!' she thought for the second time that day.

Later in the week, Tante Agathe mentioned that Philippe had suggested they should have a luncheon party.

'We've done very little to entertain you, Brianna, and

though you're Isabelle's sister, you're a guest too, and a visitor to our country.'

Well, that was true, and Brianna thought it likely she would soon be leaving Huchet-les-Anges. The latest letter from Switzerland had said that Maman was fast regaining her health and strength and hoped to be home in two more weeks. Two more weeks! And then Brianna would leave Burgundy and Philippe and Tante Agathe and join her mother in Paris. She wasn't sure if she was glad or not that the time for departure was beginning to loom up, and when, after the contents of the letter had been made known, Philippe got her alone and asked her, 'Are you hoping the next two weeks will speed by, *belle-soeur*?' she hardly knew what to say. So many things had begun—so many things that she suspected she might never see ended.

'I'm content to wait here till Maman is quite well. Why do you ask?'

He smiled sardonically. 'I'm trying to figure out whether you're more eager to stay here in the vicinity of your latest admirer, or hasten the time when you can return home to your older one.'

'Neither one of them enters my calculations,' she said, flushing. 'I've already told you I have no thoughts of marriage.'

'And I don't believe you,' he said calmly. 'All girls have thoughts of marriage in their heads, from when they're still well and truly at school.'

'I'm afraid you're out of date. Marriage is no longer the favourite daydream.'

'Perhaps not. But if marriage isn't your favourite daydream, you must put another ambition in its place. What would that be? You don't strike me as being a career girl, you haven't shown any signs of becoming a dedicated world traveller, and neither can I see you happy in a relationship with a man without making it legal.'

Brianna shrugged and turned away. She wanted to get married and have children, but she wasn't going to tell *him* that ...

And now a luncheon party was being planned to entertain her.

'Who are the guests to be?' she asked Tante Agathe, while they were all out in the garden. They would be Albertine and Louis Moreau, and the English cousin, Richard Hazelwood, Tante Agathe told her. She went on to plan the menu, and Isabelle surprisingly started offering suggestions, though Marie-Claude, who was cutting some roses, didn't take a hand.

'Brioches-Roquefort for the hors d'oeuvres,' Tante Agathe decided, 'and then chicken, perhaps——'

'With mushrooms!' put in Isabelle, her dark eyes sparkling. 'Bertine just adores mushrooms!'

'Very well then—with mushrooms, and a dish of salad,' Tante Agathe conceded. 'And we'll have Philippe's favourite dessert, a chocolate mousse flavoured with crushed almonds. I'll have Violette bring us some cream from the farm, and we'll leave the wines to Philippe.'

'I'm going to ask if we can have champagne for the aperitif,' Isabelle said dreamily. 'Champagne I adore.'

'I shall tell Violette before she leaves this morning that I want her to stay and help tomorrow,' Tante Agathe stated, ignoring this remark. 'She will mind the children while we have *déjeuner*, and clear up afterwards.'

Brianna went to bed that night feeling slightly keyed up. It wasn't the fact that they were to have a luncheon party, she admitted to herself. It was because she was going to meet Bertine again, and that was rather odd. But she wanted to decide for herself what Philippe felt for the girl. His manner towards her would surely be revealing, and if he was possessive, openly affectionate, then she would conclude that Isabelle's opinions had been a lot of nonsense.

Certainly Philippe was always scolding her for talking too much about other people's business!

It may have been the fact that she was tensed up and so slept lightly, but she wakened in the morning when it was scarcely light, her heart pounding. What had disturbed her? some sound——

She sat up in bed and listened. Was that the soft brush of footsteps in the hall or on the stairs? Could it be Olympe awake and bent on mischief? The child had made an early morning visit to the kitchen once before and spilt a whole jug of milk on the floor.

Brianna slid out of bed and slipped on her blue and lilac gown. Then without bothering to put on her slippers, she went into the hall. Not a sign of anyone—not a sound. Quietly she went down the stairs, and as she reached the foot of them she heard stealthy sounds coming from the direction of the kitchen. So it was Olympe!

But it was not the child. Reaching the kitchen, she discovered Isabelle there—fully dressed in jeans, a long-sleeved dark shirt and—boots! She was helping herself quietly to bread and had already poured herself a glass of fruit juice.

Her face reddened with guilt as she swung round to find Brianna there.

'What on earth are you up to, Isabelle?' Brianna asked. 'Where do you plan to go—in those boots?'

Isabelle drank down half the glass of fruit juice before she answered. Then she said aggressively, 'I'll tell you, Brianna—though I don't have to, you know. It's none of your business. I'm going to the fields to gather mushrooms.'

Brianna stared at her and in a flash she had interpreted that guilty look.

'You're going with Emile Dupont,' she accused.

'Yes.' Her sister's eyes were bright. 'He knows where the

best mushrooms are to be found. He told me so that day at the farm.'

'You've been seeing him, then, to have arranged this.'

Isabelle scowled at her. 'How officious and disapproving you sound! Just like Philippe. But suppose I have, where's the harm?'

Brianna opened her mouth to speak, but Isabelle continued quickly, 'I haven't seen him, anyhow, so don't lecture me. I sent a message to him yesterday, by Violette, asking him to meet me. He'll come,' she added complacently, and took a healthy bite from the long roll of bread she had split and buttered for herself.

Brianna swallowed nervously. There was something disturbing about the way Isabelle had said, 'He'll come'. It was as if she saw Emile as something rather more than a companion with whom to go mushrooming. Brianna remembered with sudden clarity how she had said that day as they came home from the farm, 'He's just so sexy—I get the loveliest feeling all through my body'.

She bit her lip. 'I don't think you should go. It's not necessary—Tante Agathe intends to buy mushrooms in the village this morning. Besides,' she finished warningly, 'Philippe will be furious. You know what he said.'

Isabelle laughed. 'Pouf! What do I care if Philippe is angry? I'm used to it. I don't intend to be treated like an infant all my life, anyhow. I don't feel even two days younger than Bertine, who is nineteen though she doesn't look it. Philippe doesn't treat *her* as a child, though I daresay she'd obey even his slightest command. But me, I shall do as I like. What are you going to do about it? Are you going to wake Philippe and tell tales on me?'

That, of course, was exactly what Brianna should do and she knew it. But she knew too that she simply couldn't do it. She couldn't—go over to the other side.

'No, of course I'm not,' she told her sister, slowly. 'I'm

just going to ask you to use your sense and not to go. Emile is——'

Isabelle sent her a wide-eyed innocent look. 'Emile is what, Brianna? You said before that there was no harm in my going mushrooming with him, and there isn't. I can't see why you should change your mind. I like him—and I want to go mushrooming. I'm tired of doing nothing more exciting than minding the children and taking them for walks and playing croquet on the lawn. Everything will be all right. Tell Philippe if you like—when he comes down to breakfast. I must go now, or I'll be late.' She sent Brianna a rather malicious smile and was gone.

Brianna had little choice but to let her go, and after all, she argued with herself, where was the harm? She remembered uneasily what Philippe had said that night—that Emile wouldn't even try to resist a girl as attractive as Isabelle. But—out in the fields in the morning? It was too silly to contemplate. A kiss, perhaps, but that would be all. And after all, Brianna assured herself, seeing his sister worked for the d'Helliers, he would have more sense than to stir up trouble for himself. Everything would be all right. She went back up the stairs to her bed.

It was still a tremendous relief when Isabelle arrived home at about breakfast time. Marie-Claude had not yet come down, but the others were seated at the table, and Brianna, knowing it was assumed Isabelle was still in bed, had said nothing to enlighten anybody.

Then in came Isabelle, her boots muddy, her cheeks flushed, carrying a small sack that Brianna at least knew was filled with mushrooms. She dumped it on the floor with a triumphant and slightly defiant, 'There's my contribution to the party—some lovely fresh mushrooms!'

Philippe glared at her, his sapphire eyes narrowed.

'What the devil have you been up to? I thought you were still upstairs.'

Isabelle quailed slightly but said boldly, 'Me? I've been up for hours! Didn't Brianna tell you? We thought we'd surprise Tante Agathe and bring some mushrooms home, but Brianna decided it was too early for her to leave her bed.'

Brianna felt the colour rush to her face. She could hardly believe her ears. Isabelle was trying to make her a willing accessory—when she had been a most unwilling one! And she didn't for a minute think that Philippe would take it that Isabelle had gone out on her own.

He shot Brianna an angry look. 'If she'd told me what you were up to I'd have taken the car and flushed you out, you little idiot. You've been with that peasant, of course.'

'Oh, Philippe!' Isabelle exclaimed with a pout, her colour deepening with excitement rather than with fear or remorse. 'I wish you wouldn't keep calling Emile a peasant that way. He's very nice—I like him.' She moved a little to rest one hand on the sideboard while she pulled off her muddy boots, oblivious of the mess they made on the clean floor, and of Tante Agathe's look of displeasure. 'He knows all about the country—he knows exactly where to go for the biggest mushrooms.' She poked at the sack with the toe of one foot, and revealed a tumble of earthy-smelling mushrooms. 'These are marvellous. Can't you smell them? Don't they make your mouth water?'

Philippe ignored this red herring.

'If you were just a little younger, Isabelle, I'd put you across my knee and give you a good spanking.'

'But I'm not younger after all, am I, Philippe?' Isabelle up.' She stood looking at him challengingly and Brianna wouldn't have blamed him in the least if he'd got up there and then and delivered the spanking despite her sixteen years.

For a moment it seemed that was exactly what he was going to do, and Isabelle stood waiting, looking very small and very young without her boots, smiling almost as though she wanted it to happen. *Did* she? Did she want Philippe to spank her? The thought turned Brianna's stomach very slightly. She was relieved when he didn't move from his chair after all. Instead, he swallowed down his rage with a visible effort and said coldly, 'If I'm to have no authority over you, Isabelle, you won't come to Huchet-les-Anges for a holiday ever again. I promise you that. Just watch your step in future.'

'Oh, Philippe! You could never be so unfair! Maman would never allow it—and I did it all for you! Poor Bertine adores mushrooms. Don't you want to please her?'

'Poor Bertine will be equally satisfied, whatever she gets here,' he said irritably, and Brianna caught her breath at something in his tone. He sounded so utterly callous, as though the mere thought of Bertine bored him. Moreover, she was sure he wasn't referring to mushrooms or to food of any kind. He was referring to his treatment of her—to her admiration for him. Oh, he was a heartless man! She would hate and loathe to be emotionally involved with him in any way at all. Yet they were already emotionally involved—but the emotion was that of dislike, not, thank heaven, of love.

Philippe went ahead and finished his coffee and rolls, ignoring both Isabelle and Brianna, and instead discussing with Tante Agathe the idea of lunching al fresco.

'Violette can help me carry the table outside—she's a strong young woman,' he said.

Brianna was tidying her bedroom some time later when he came into the room unceremoniously and stood, hands on hips, watching her forbiddingly as she straightened the blue bedspread.

'You're a bad influence on your young sister, with your crackpot ideas about innocence, *belle-soeur*,' he remarked. 'You could at least have gone with the child this morning.'

Brianna considered telling him she had known nothing of the proposed expedition until it was too late, but decided against it. She didn't want to tell tales on Isabelle and cause more trouble.

'Oh, you're making a fuss about nothing,' she told him dismissively. 'She's home quite safe and sound, and it's a pity to spoil her pleasure.'

His blue eyes flashed at her. 'There's pleasure and pleasure, *chérie*—and some pleasures have a very bitter aftermath. I don't want Isabelle to experience *that* particular kind of pleasure too young—and don't give me that blank look, you know very well what I'm talking about. I've already indicated to you, since you aren't sharp enough to work it out for yourself, that your sister's not exactly undersexed, nor is Emile Dupont. He's a devil—he's not like the other boys in the Dupont family, but he's the one Isabelle has her eye on.'

Brianna left the bed and went to move things aimlessly about on the dressing table. She hated Philippe for talking like that. She was positive that Isabelle was just a nice normal girl—a little lively—whose head was full of romantic notions. It was horrible of him to colour them with the cynicism of sophistication.

'I warn you,' he said, after a brief silence, 'if you don't co-operate with me in disciplining Isabelle—and it's all for her own good, remember—I shall have no hesitation in asking you to leave my house.'

She swung round to face him, breathing deeply. He was insufferable! 'I shall—I shall have no hesitation in going, *beau-frère*,' she told him. 'The way I see it, you're trying to poison innocence, and I don't want to ally myself with you.'

His eyes sparked angrily. 'Then don't ally yourself with Emile Dupont,' he said curtly, and left the room.

After that, Brianna was not really in the mood to enjoy the day's festivities, though rather surprisingly Isabelle and Philippe seemed perfectly as usual. She herself felt angry with Isabelle for involving her, with Philippe for blaming her, and with herself for taking a stand that she was beginning to doubt. She knew in her heart that she didn't want to be asked to leave Philippe's house, not only for her mother's sake, but for her own. Maman would be upset if there was another storm over Brianna, and besides, she was beginning to like it here, though heaven knew why . . .

The luncheon party started with champagne and pretzels under the trees, and then everyone moved to the big farm table that had been set up in the shade near the house. It was covered with a hand-crocheted cloth, and adorned with a low earthen bowl full of wild flowers, gathered in the forest by Marie-Claude. Philippe took the head of the table with Bertine on one side of him and Isabelle on the other. Tante Agathe was at the foot flanked by Marie-Claude and Richard, while Louis and Brianna sat opposite each other in a middle position, and Brianna had Richard and Bertine at either side of her.

It may have been the champagne, or the good red wine from Philippe's own vineyards, but Isabelle seemed intent on making herself the centre of attention and on distracting Philippe from Bertine. She complained that the hors d'oeuvres—brioches filled with a delicious mixture of Roquefort cheese, cream and egg yolks—was too rich for her.

'Philippe—Philippe—would you like my portion? I shall be ill if I eat all this.'

'Then leave it, *chérie*,' he said tolerantly. 'I'm well satisfied with what I have.'

But she didn't leave it, Brianna noticed, she ate it all up
with great relish. And when the chicken and mushrooms
were passed around, and Bertine rather shyly admitted her
partiality for mushrooms, Isabelle broke into giggles which
she hid behind her hand.

'Oh, don't bring up the subject of the mushrooms, Bertine—Philippe's very cross with me for going out to gather
those, aren't you, Philippe?'

Brianna, trying to give her attention to Richard, longed
to tell her sister to be quiet, and wondered that for once
Philippe didn't do so, but let her babble on as much as she
liked. To Bertine he was polite and kind, but that was all,
and Brianna felt thoughtful. The young French girl was
obviously more than a little in awe of him, and the expression in her rather innocent eyes, as she listened intently to
everything he said to her, revealed with painful clarity that
she looked up to him as to some god. With Bertine, Brianna
found herself thinking, the harvest was certainly ready to
be gathered. But would he marry her? She certainly wasn't
the type who would make a fuss, no matter what he did. If
he had a mistress, for instance—Brianna was somewhat
shocked at her own thoughts, but she had gradually reached
the conclusion that the other girl, if she existed, must
already be married. That was the only explanation for the
secrecy, and for the fact that Philippe was still a bachelor.

But perhaps the wine was going to her head too, and she
turned away from her contemplation of Bertine to listen to
what Richard was telling her.

'I've been trying to get the use of Grand'mère's car so
we can go to Armette and get that painting framed,
Brianna. You'll come with me, won't you? I'm pretty sure
I can manage it on Tuesday—keep that day free.'

'Yes, of course I'll do that,' Brianna agreed brightly. She

reflected wryly that she didn't have all that many social engagements and would have made some light remark to that effect to Richard except that her attention would keep straying to that silly little sister of hers who was busy once more putting poor Bertine's nose out of joint.

It wasn't till later when coffee had been served at the small table, and Violette was clearing away the dishes, that she noticed how quiet Marie-Claude and Louis had been. They were not behaving at all like a couple who were soon to become engaged. In fact, she thought, glancing at them as she helped herself to sugar, Louis was looking distinctly bored while Marie-Claude, through half closed eyes, quite plainly had her attention riveted on Richard, who had scarcely spoken to her. She left the small group presently and followed Tante Agathe inside to ask if there was anything she could do to help.

'No, *ma chère*. Violette will do everything that needs to be done. I myself mean to go upstairs and have a rest with the children. You young people are free to amuse yourselves.'

When Brianna went outside again, Marie-Claude and Richard were talking to each other, both of them looking somewhat guilty. Philippe and Louis were engaged in a discussion, no doubt concerned with wine growing, and the other two girls sat listening, and taking no notice of each other.

Brianna stood hesitating, not certain which group she should join, then Marie-Claude suggested a game of croquet.

What was left of the afternoon passed quickly, and soon the guests were leaving while the others came to the gate to say a last farewell—almost as if they were seeing them off on a long journey, thought Brianna. They had barely gone when a disreputable old Renault came rattling along the street and pulled up, and out stepped Emile Dupont.

Isabelle blushed scarlet and giggled behind her hand, 'He's come to fetch Violette—he promised he would.'

Philippe gave her a steely look. 'Then he can wait out here for Violette. As for you, run along inside. All of you,' he added briskly. 'Get a move on now, Isabelle, or I shall use force.'

'Pig!' Isabelle muttered, but she went inside and so did Marie-Claude.

But Brianna did not. She stayed where she was. She was English and she wasn't going to be bossed about by Philippe as though she were one of his young sisters. Besides, she wanted to take another look at Emile Dupont and decide for herself if he was as much of a menace as Philippe claimed him to be.

Philippe, as if she simply wasn't there, strode across the street where he stood talking to the young farm boy, who leaned against the door of his car in an indolent manner.

'I suppose he's telling him to leave Isabelle alone,' Brianna thought, watching from afar. Certainly Emile was very good-looking in a rough and swarthy way, and certainly he was very, very masculine. There was an earthiness about him, a boldness, and even from here she was aware of his sensuality. A vivid picture came back into her mind, of how he had stood so close to Isabelle at the farm, his body curved, his hips jutting, his head bent to hers while she laughed up at him. He was scowling now and looking at Philippe in a belligerent, sullen way. Then quite abruptly, having said what he wanted, Philippe turned away and came back towards Brianna. He looked very handsome and very angry, and Brianna felt a shiver run down her spine.

'Are you *still* here?' Philippe said sharply. 'I told you to go inside.'

'I know you did. But I don't happen to want to go inside yet. I—I want to tell that boy that we enjoyed the mushrooms,' she heard herself say defiantly, though she hadn't planned to do any such thing. 'I can see you've been insulting him, and all he's done is help Isabelle gather mushrooms.'

Philippe caught her savagely by the arm. 'You sound very sure of yourself—but if you want the truth, Isabelle's already admitted he kissed her.'

'Oh, really, Philippe! Is that so frightful? What girl hasn't been kissed at sixteen?' She pulled away from his grasp and marched past him and across the street. She was shaken, but she wasn't going to let Philippe see it. And she was determined—*determined* to speak to Emile, to prove to herself that Philippe was being over-protective, that Emile Dupont was nothing but a harmless young man like any other boy of his age.

Emile had lit a cigarette and he watched her progress through half-closed, bold black eyes, an indolent smile on his lips. Brianna forced herself to look straight at him—a long searching look—and to answer his smile with a bright one of her own.

'Oh, Emile, I wanted to tell you how good the mushrooms were. We enjoyed them so much. It was very kind of you to take my sister to gather them.'

His smile broadened and he muttered something that she found quite unintelligible. She said hesitantly, 'I beg your pardon, I—I don't understand what you're saying. My French isn't very good.'

His glance roamed over her openly, and she had a horrible feeling that she was being stripped. Then he said slowly and carefully, 'I'd like to take *you* mushrooming some time—preferably in the evening.' What followed that, she only understood in part, but it was enough to make the colour leave her face. With a tremendous effort she made herself look back at him and tell him coldly, 'I'm afraid I don't understand. But it doesn't matter ... Thank you again.'

She left him quickly. Her ears were burning and her knees were shaking. To her relief, Philippe wasn't waiting for her in the garden, and she didn't go inside, but simply stood in the shade, trying to compose herself and to get rid of the sick feeling in her stomach.

The things Emile had said—the way he had looked at her just now—made her feel soiled and utterly ashamed. Oh God! She hoped he hadn't talked that way to her little sister! And if having him look at her in that—*obscene* way gave her what she had called 'the loveliest feeling' all through her body, then the thrill she got was not so harmless after all.

Yes, undoubtedly Philippe was right. Isabelle badly needed to be protected, both from herself and from this peasant, before she rushed headlong into disaster. And Brianna, who found it so unpalatable to take orders from him, knew that in future, at least where Isabelle was concerned, she would co-operate with him to the full. Not because she didn't want to be asked to leave his house, but for Isabelle's sake.

CHAPTER SEVEN

THAT little incident was the beginning of a changed relationship between herself and Philippe, though Brianna didn't realise it until much later.

In bed that night, she did a little soul-searching and somewhat reluctantly came to the conclusion that Philippe had been quite right when he had said he knew Isabelle a hundred times better than she did. She *didn't* know or understand Isabelle, and she had been so intent on her feud with Philippe that, quite honestly, she hadn't thought about her sister a great deal. Yet her whole idea in coming to France had been to build up a good relationship with her own family and with the d'Helliers, who were so important in their lives. But what a mess she was making of it! Certainly she had been able to help with the children, but in all her encounters with Philippe she had behaved like a spoilt child, and been intent on scoring off him. He must now be convinced that his opinion of her, based on her past performance, was thoroughly justified, and once again she had reason to be ashamed of herself.

The truth was, she mused, staring into the darkness, that her personal antagonism to Philippe, too, was based on what was long over and done with. In other words, she was no better than he was when it came to forgetting the past. Before she slept, she resolved to smarten herself up, to think before she suspected Philippe's motives or took offence at anything he might do or say. To behave, in effect, like the mature and fair-minded person she had pretended to herself she had become. That, she realised, would mean admitting to Philippe that she had been wrong. It would mean apologising to him.

Well then, she would do it. She would do it if it killed her.

But it didn't kill her. In fact, to begin with, it proved to be not an unpleasant experience at all.

By loitering in the garden the following evening, she managed to get Philippe to herself for a few minutes when he came home from the vineyards, and as soon as he had garaged his car she approached him directly.

'Philippe——'

'Yes?' He was walking towards the house, but he halted and looked down at her enquiringly, his eyes screwed up a little. It struck her suddenly that his face had become almost unbearably familiar to her, and as their eyes met she felt an odd quickening of her pulses. Something in his way of looking at her, something that seemed new—warm, intimate, meaningful—stirred her so that her breath came fast, and she remembered vividly his accusations that she had stirred Richard up simply by looking at him. Now he was doing the same to her——

His lips curved faintly and his brows rose as he reached out and closed his fingers around her wrist.

'Well? What is it you want to say to me, *ma chère*?'

She swallowed and with an effort pulled herself together.

'Just that—I'm sorry about yesterday. About having been so—obtuse. You're quite right about Emile—I admit it. He's no sort of companion for Isabelle and I promise I shan't encourage her to see him again. So you won't have to send her away,' she finished with a nervous laugh.

His fingers tightened on her wrist. 'You don't want to be sent away, then? You wouldn't care as little as you pretended?'

She shook her head, and now her eyes had gone to his lips—to that curving sensual mouth that belied the asceticism of his brow, and that had, not so many days ago, aroused her in a way she had never been roused before, little though she had been prepared to admit it at the time.

'No, I—I don't want to go, Philippe,' she murmured.
And immediately wondered what she had confessed—to
herself, and to him.

'Funnily enough, I don't want you to go either,' he said,
and his voice was low too and there was an odd vibration
in it. Then almost immediately, he withdrew his hand from
her wrist and said abruptly, 'I'm gratified you recognise the
sense in what I said, Brianna.' He began to move towards
the house. 'Have you amused yourself today? Did you see
Richard Hazelwood?'

'No.' She felt rebuffed. 'We're meeting on Tuesday. He's
making me a gift of one of his paintings, and we're going
to Armette to arrange to have it framed.'

'Congratulations,' he said dryly. 'I hope it's worth framing.'

'It is. Richard has a great deal of talent—I'm sure of it.'

He made no further comment but held the door open for
her and followed her through the big hallway and into the
living room, where the rest of the family was gathered.
Isabelle, giving Jean-Christian his *biberon*, flashed her eyes
at Brianna angrily.

'I thought you were to feed *bébé* tonight.'

'It appears you were wrong, then, Isabelle,' Philippe
flung himself down on the settee with its deerskin cover as
he spoke. 'You've been too idle for your own good lately,
and idleness leads to mischief ... Brianna's been telling me
about Richard Hazelwood's talents as an artist,' he continued to the room at large. 'What's the subject of this
painting you're to be given, *belle-soeur*?'

The mockery, the hard antagonism were back in his eyes
and in his voice, and she felt helpless. It was all very well to
make good resolutions, but he would have to make some
too before there would be peace between them.

'It's a picture of sunflowers,' she said, the coolness of

her tone indicating that she didn't intend to go into details for his benefit. 'I'll show it to you when it's been framed.' She turned away in search of something to do to help. Tante Agathe was supervising Olympe's supper, and Marie-Claude, who had been spreading the cloth on the big table, had for some reason left it half done, and was now at the sideboard, with her back to Brianna.

Brianna carefully straightened the cloth, and when Marie-Claude turned back with a handful of cutlery and smiled at her, she thought it was a peculiarly strained smile. Marie-Claude's voice was strained too as she said pleasantly, 'I should like to see the picture too, Brianna. I have never seen any of Richard's paintings.'

On Tuesday, Richard managed to borrow his grandmother's car, and he and Brianna went to Armette. Then, before returning home, they went to the pavement café for a drink. After the waiter had brought their coffee, Richard asked casually, running his fingers through his fair hair, 'How's Marie-Claude these days?'

She looked at him in surprise. 'She's perfectly well. What do you mean?'

'Well—since the break-up. She hasn't said anything about it to you?'

'No. But do you mean that she and Louis have—have parted company?'

'That's about it. Didn't you notice at lunch the other day, they hardly exchanged a word? I asked Louis what was going on, and he said the romance was all off. I don't think Grand'mère's been told yet. She'll hit the roof when she knows. It's as well *she* wasn't at the party, what with Louis and Marie-Claude being so bored with each other, and that sexy young sister of yours trying her best to trespass on Bertine's preserves——'

Brianna stared at him. 'Whatever are you talking about?' she asked, flushing.

His expression was quizzical. 'Oh, my dear girl—of course you know that Grand'mère has her eye on the d'Helliers as a means of bringing a little money to the rescue of the manor house! It's not only Marie-Claude she wants, it's Philippe as well. There aren't too many bright young girls around in a tiny village like Huchet, you know, and someone as pretty and charming as Bertine should be well in the running to win him. It's unfortunate the poor kid doesn't know any of the tricks—whereas young Isabelle obviously knows the lot! Now Bertine's so down in the dumps she wants to go home to Armette—she told me so herself. And it's thanks to Isabelle.'

'Oh, really!' Brianna exclaimed, annoyed. 'You can't blame Isabelle for that. You're quite wrong about her, I assure you. I know she was being very naughty the other day, but——'

'Naughty!' Richard echoed, raising his eyebrows in an exaggerated show of amazement. 'What a way of putting it! —though it depends how you mean the word. I know she's your young sister, but frankly I think she's a very dangerous little flirt, and so possessive of Philippe it's nobody's business. She doesn't intend Bertine to have him. She really meant business the other day.'

'That's ridiculous!' Brianna felt more annoyed than ever. 'Isabelle's a schoolgirl. I know she likes to torment Philippe, but—but he's like a brother to her.'

Richard laughed softly and mockingly. 'Come on now, Brianna! Face the facts! After all, he's not her brother. Is he like a brother to you?'

Her colour deepened. 'That's quite different. Isabelle's been part of the d'Hellier family since she was quite small. You've got it all wrong. But let's not argue. Anyhow, do you think Bertine's really in love with Philippe?'

He spread his hands in a French-looking gesture. 'I doubt whether Bertine knows what love is yet. She's quietly waiting to find out. And while as a nicely brought up young French girl she has a lot of respect for Grand'mère's wishes, I think if it came to the point she'd be frightened out of her wits if Philippe took it into his head to teach her. He wants a tiger—and she's a kitten. The game would be too rough for her. Grand'mère's made a mistake, in my opinion.' He pushed back his chair a little. 'Well, we'd better be getting back to Huchet and put an end to this session of scandal-mongering. Grand'mère will think I'm busily seducing you—though it probably wouldn't bother her all that much if I was.' He hesitated and looked a little uncomfortable. 'There's something else I want to talk about though, Brianna. Look, now that Marie-Claude and Louis are through—well, don't laugh—but I might make a bid for her myself. I don't know what my chances would be. The d'Helliers aren't noted for their fondness for the English, are they? I'm being tactless, aren't I? Let's put it this way—their preferences definitely are for the French.'

Brianna smiled slightly. 'Don't try to spare my feelings.' His disclosure surprised her, yet as her mind flipped rapidly back she could see the signs had possibly been there right from the start. She told him cheerfully, 'Marie-Claude's interested in England anyhow, and she's been working hard practising her English, if that's any comfort to you. I really don't think she has much against us.'

'Well, that's a ray of hope,' he said lightly. 'You're a good sport, Brianna. Here I've been, making passes at you, and now I'm telling you I have heavy leanings towards some other female! You must think me a rotten type. Does that smiling exterior hide a broken heart?'

'You know it doesn't,' she said with a smile.

'Now *I'm* hurt,' he grinned back at her. 'But actually I always had the feeling a girl as bright as you must have a boy-friend tucked away somewhere back in England. Am I right?'

She grimaced. 'I'm sorry—no. It seems to be a popular idea with everyone, but I'm completely fancy free and happy to be that way.' As she spoke, she had an odd sense of having said something not strictly true, and she hastened on, not pausing to examine the slightly disquieting notion, 'I'll make it clear to Marie-Claude that you're not in any way my property, anyhow. Come to think of it, I don't think she was terribly pleased when she knew you'd given me a painting, though she hid it pretty well. But that's something you'll have to find out for yourself, isn't it?'

'It is—and I'll get to work on it,' he said, and they exchanged smiles with each other.

Philippe arrived back from the vineyard just as Richard was letting Brianna out of his car and telling her, 'I shan't come in now—I have to get this vehicle back. But I'll be around, be sure of it.' With a wave he was off, and Brianna went inside with Philippe, who had waited for her.

'The platonic friendship seems to be thriving,' he remarked sardonically.

'Actually it is,' she agreed, and sent him an innocent smile.

'You'll be sorry when the time comes to leave for Paris.'

'Yes, I shall,' she agreed, and meant it, though it was not on Richard's account.

Next day's mail brought two items of news. There was to be a slight delay in Maman's return, and Paul and Micheline would be arriving in Huchet-les-Anges in two days' time to collect the children and take them home to Dijon.

'What a relief it will be to be rid of those little pests,' Isabelle remarked that afternoon. The three girls were in the garden, where Olympe was playing with her dolls. Tante Agathe had taken Jean-Christian with her to the village where she had some shopping to do, and Philippe had not been home since shortly after breakfast. 'No more *biberons* to prepare or dreary dawdling walks to go,' Isabelle continued, and looked across at Brianna, her face thoughtful. 'You won't be needed here any more, Brianna. You might as well go back home to England, mightn't you?'

Brianna flinched slightly, hurt by her sister's tone.

'I must see Maman when she comes back, Isabelle,' she said quietly.

'Pouf! How can you expect anyone to believe you care about that after all the years when you took no notice of us? But you can wait in England as well as you can wait here, I should think. Why don't you get your boy-friend to bring you to Paris later in the year?'

'Because Peter and I don't have that kind of friendship,' Brianna said tartly.

'I suppose that's because of Richard Hazelwood,' Isabelle commented.

'Well, it's not. Richard and I are only friends.'

'I don't believe it.' Isabelle jumped up from the grass restlessly. 'I'm tired of doing nothing. I'm going to cycle out to Les Fleurons.' She vaulted over the balustrade and crossed the flagged court to the garage to reappear presently wheeling a bicycle. Brianna, who had followed her, stopped her near the gate.

'*Are* you going to Les Fleurons, Isabelle?' she asked worriedly.

Her sister looked back at her impudently, her black eyes sparkling. 'Yes, I am—and don't offer to come with me. I don't want your company.'

Brianna flushed. 'I wasn't going to offer it. I just want to make sure you're not going to the Duponts' farm.'

'Oh!' Isabelle covered her mouth with one hand to hide a giggle. 'You think I'm looking for Emile Dupont! Well, I'm not.' She flipped her fingers. 'I don't care *that* for Emile

Dupont just now—I'd completely forgotten him. I want to
be first to tell Philippe all the news about Paul and
Micheline and Maman. We'll see what *he* has to say about
your staying on now Maman's return has been delayed,
and the infants will be gone. Do you know it was only for
Maman's sake he asked you here? We don't usually take
strangers into our homes—and nobody wanted you to
come.'

Brianna bit her lip. 'You don't mean that, Isabelle. I'm
not a stranger—I'm your sister. What's got into you that
you should suddenly say such things to me?' she finished,
her voice trembling a little.

'Oh, now I've hurt your feelings.' Isabelle didn't sound
as if she cared in the least if she had. 'But I'm only telling
you the truth. Philippe said we must all be nice to you, but
no one ever dreamed you'd be staying so long. You've spoilt
the summer for us, you know—Philippe's been bad-
tempered, and nothing's been the same. We all just wish
you'd go away and leave us to live our own lives,' she concluded, her eyes flashing with malice. Then, her outburst
over, she swung herself on to her bicycle and with a toss of
her pigtails sailed away.

Brianna stood where she was, her heart racing, her
thoughts in a turmoil. Isabelle sounded as if she actually
disliked her! But why? *Why?* Oh, how true it was that she
didn't know her own sister! Philippe had told her so, and
even Richard had implied it when he had said Isabelle knew
all the tricks, and that it was her fault Bertine wanted to go
home to Armette. Now, quite shockingly, it seemed she
wanted to be rid of Brianna too. Again—why? Did she—
could she—want Philippe to herself? If the children went
—if Marie-Claude went—if Brianna were to be banished
—then Isabelle and Philippe would be alone, but for Tante
Agathe. Was *that* what her sister wanted?

'I'm mad!' Brianna interrupted her own thoughts impatiently. There was another girl: Isabelle had said so. Besides, Isabelle was only sixteen. 'Sixteen and very, very pretty.' Philippe had said that in Canterbury.

Rather slowly and thoughtfully, she made her way back to Marie-Claude, pausing to check that Olympe, who was singing to herself as she changed her dolls' clothes, and struggling patiently with buttons, wasn't in need of attention.

Marie-Claude sat where she had left her, looking rather pensive.

'What were we talking about?' Brianna asked with an effort at brightness as she sat down on the grass. She tried to ignore the clamour of her thoughts, and the insistent inner voice that told her over and over, 'I don't want to go —not before I've made some kind of peace with Philippe.'

'We were speaking of your English friend,' Marie-Claude said. 'And of—of Richard.'

'Yes, of course. And I'm afraid I was irritated by Isabelle's suppositions. The fact is, there's absolutely no question of a romance between Richard and myself. We have something in common because we were both brought up in England and that's all there is to it.'

'Yes? But he's made you a gift of one of his paintings,' Marie-Claude rejoined. There was a tinge of extra bright colour in her cheeks and her eyes were wary. Brianna began to wonder seriously if her change of feelings towards Louis had something definite to do with Richard. As she had told Richard, her stepsister showed a great deal of interest in England, and as she had promised to make sure Marie-Claude knew she had no claim on him, she told her, with regard to Richard's gift, 'That was only because I admired his work. And actually I'm not at all sure I should accept it. He really shouldn't give away his pictures like that. Perhaps I'll hang it in the house here, if Philippe will allow it. Anyhow—we shall see when it's been collected from the framers.'

'When will that be?' For all her casualness, there was an edge of tension to Marie-Claude's voice.

Brianna shrugged. 'I have no idea. Richard will see to it ... Apparently Bertine is talking about going back to Armette, so perhaps he'll go when Louis drives her home—and I expect you'll be invited along too,' she added deliberately.

Marie-Claude dropped her lashes. 'You mean by Louis? No, Brianna, that's very unlikely. You might as well know, I've told Philippe and it's not a secret. Louis and I have ended our friendship. We no longer think of marrying. It was taken for granted we were in love, and I suppose we were a little. We saw so much of each other when I came to Huchet-les-Anges. Madame Hubert-Benoise would invite me to the *manoir* and always Louis was there, and he is very handsome and it is such a beautiful house. One day it will belong to Louis, Madame Hubert-Benoise tells me. She would very much like us to marry, and Philippe approved. I like to please people, to do the right thing.' She smiled a little sadly. 'So Louis and I—we kiss, we talk seriously, he tells me about the vines, about the wines he makes, and we enjoy each other's company. But now' —she shrugged in the French way—'it's all over between us, that's all. So you see, I shan't be going to Armette with him, and I don't think I shall come again to Huchet for a very long time. When Micheline and Paul come tomorrow, I'll go back to Dijon with them. It's the tactful thing to do.'

'Oh no, you mustn't do that,' Brianna exclaimed.

'No? But you and I understand each other now—we will part good friends, just as Philippe wished.'

'Yes, but——' Brianna broke off. Richard Hazelwood

had appeared and was crossing the courtyard towards them. He could plead his own cause.

But Marie-Claude, whose face had paled, was getting to her feet.

'Don't go,' Brianna said quickly. 'Richard and I don't want to be left alone with each other. Please!'

Marie-Claude sat down again, and it was Brianna who jumped up from the grass and, catching Olympe's eyes, indicated that the child was to come to her. When Richard joined them, she remarked as soon as they had greeted each other, 'Olympe and I are going inside to read a story from a fairytale book. Aren't we, *chérie?*'

Marie-Claude looked dismayed. 'Oh, please—Richard will want to arrange with you about the painting.'

'The painting?' Richard obviously had to make an effort to switch his thoughts to that subject. 'Oh yes, I'm to pick it up tomorrow. Why don't you two girls come to Armette with me?'

'I can't come,' Brianna said at once. 'Tante Agathe and I have—er—plans for tomorrow,' she added vaguely.

'Marie-Claude?'

The French girl hesitated. 'I don't know. I shall go to Dijon with my brother the following day, Richard, and finish my holiday there.'

'Must you?'

'Yes, I think I must. I'm sure Philippe will say so.'

Brianna took hold of Olympe's hand. It was time to make herself scarce. 'Come along, Olympe—we're going to read the story of the Sleeping Beauty.'

She disappeared rapidly inside with a parting smile at Richard.

She was sitting on the sofa in the living room some time later, the child ensconced on her knee as they pored over the storybook together, when she heard the sound of

Isabelle's voice as she came into the house, and then her footsteps as she ran upstairs. The next minute, Philippe came into the room and stood looking down at her frowningly.

'Don't you know Richard Hazelwood's outside in the garden?' he asked her bluntly.

She looked at him over Olympe's dark head. 'Yes, I know. He's talking to Marie-Claude, isn't he?'

'Hadn't you better go out?'

'Me? Why?' She widened her eyes, then seting the expression in his, dropped her lashes with a feeling of confusion.

'Why? Because—presumably—he's come to see you, that's why.'

'But he hasn't,' she contradicted him. 'He's come to see Marie-Claude.'

'What?' He was looking at her narrowly through blindingly sapphire eyes, and she felt a strange melting in her bones, looking back at him as he stood by the big table, in his denim pants and jacket. His hair was slightly roughened from a day outside, and his face was tanned and healthy from the sun.

'Yes,' she insisted. 'He has a right now that Marie-Claude and Louis have changed their minds about each other.'

'So that's what it's all about,' he said slowly. 'And you don't mind too much?'

'I don't mind at all. I've told you often enough it's just——'

'A platonic friendship.' He said it quizzically and his eyes went to her lips as he added deliberately, 'Well, as you know, that's something I don't believe in, Brianna.' He turned away from her momentarily to tell Olympe, who had slipped off her knee and run to the window, 'Run along outside now, *ma petite*. It will be time enough to come indoors when Tante Agathe returns.'

The child trotted off obediently, and Brianna rose nervously to her feet. The way he had looked at her just now disturbed her, and she remembered vividly how he had kissed her that evening after Madame Hubert-Benoise had warned her to stay away from him. Something had happened between them then that neither of them had wanted, and she at least had pushed the affair to the back of her mind and continued to feud with him—though not on Madame Hubert-Benoise's account! Now, somehow, the feud was over, and she wondered with a little feeling of apprehension if it wouldn't have been better—safer—to let it continue. He was going to kiss her again—she was convinced of it as she met his eyes across the room. She had a mad impulse to run away, yet at the same time she knew with a deadly certainty that she wouldn't run. In some curious way she wanted it all to happen again, just as it had happened that evening down by the stream.

Then with a start she came back to her senses. Good heavens! What was the matter? That intent look in his eyes —all it meant was that he was going to have something to say about the postponement of her mother's return to Paris! He might even be about to tell her that she had already outstayed her welcome here. Heaven alone knew what Isabelle had been saying to him, after her upsetting outburst.

She swallowed painfully then said with a hint of challenge in her voice, 'I suppose Isabelle's told you all the news?'

'Oh yes—trust Isabelle to do that ... Including the fact that you want to go back to England.'

Brianna blinked and felt her pulses quicken.

'She told you that?'

He nodded. 'Is it because it looks as if you can no longer amuse yourself with Richard Hazelwood? Or has it something to do with your—unofficial engagement in England?'

'Neither,' she said curtly. 'Besides, I don't want to go back to England.'

His eyes narrowed. 'You mean Isabelle was not telling the truth?'

Brianna hesitated. She didn't want to call her sister a liar, but all the same it had been deceitful of Isabelle. 'Perhaps Isabelle believes I want to go back,' she said at last. 'But I don't. No matter what Mrs Arden led you to believe, Peter and I are not even unofficially engaged. So you see I have nothing to go back for. I came here to see Maman, and I intend to wait in France till she returns. That is,' she added, 'if you'll allow it. I must do as you say, of course.'

His lips twisted. 'That's a surprising statement from you, *belle-soeur*. You're usually so forthright. From any other woman it would be provocative.'

She coloured. 'I don't mean to be provocative. But I'm aware I've been unnecessarily hard to get on with.'

'Not lately,' he said. 'Decidedly not ... We haven't seen a great deal of each other, actually, have we? Perhaps after the children have gone, and Marie-Claude too, we'll be able to remedy that.'

'Must Marie-Claude go?'

He frowned. 'I think so. It will save much embarrassment. Madame Hubert-Benoise is bound to be—upset about the breakdown of plans that appeared to be succeeding so well.'

'Yes, but it's not very kind to Richard,' she protested.

'To Richard! *Bon dieu,* what do you mean by that? Just because he's taken a fancy to my sister and is talking to her in the garden——'

'It's more than that. He told me so. Besides, I think Marie-Claude feels as he does.'

He made an impatient exclamation. 'Spare me from a flood of romantic suppositions! No, my sister's to go to Dijon and that's final. If Richard Hazelwood imagines he's in love with her—and you must forgive me for doubting his sincerity, since he was giving a pretty good imitation of being in love with *you* a day or so ago—then he can find his own ways and means of pursuing her. I'm not going to make it easy for him, especially as I'm more or less *in loco parentis* to Marie-Claude until my father returns to Paris.'

Brianna sighed, but said with a spark of defiance, 'It's a little funny you should talk about saving people embarrassment, seeing that you——' She stopped, biting her lip as he shot her a fiery look.

'Well, continue with what you were about to say,' he told her coolly.

'Well, seeing that Bertine wants to go back to Armette,' she said shakily. 'Richard said she does.'

He laughed mirthlessly. 'The gossip that goes on in this village! I suppose I'm being blamed for what Bertine wants and doesn't want ... *Ma chère*, you've obviously had an earful of the supposed romance between myself and Albertine Moreau—from your friend Richard, presumably. But you have no evidence that any such romance has been in progress, have you? Bertine is certainly a sweet and charming child—and an obedient one—but her prettiness doesn't go to my head, nor does my blood pound when I'm near to her. Strange as it may seem, you're the one who tantalises me, Brianna Gaze—physically always, emotionally more and more.'

She stared at him and slowly blushed scarlet. She had no real idea how to take what he had said, particularly in view of the fact that Isabelle was so insistent he was involved with some other girl. It was just a form of mild flirtation, she told herself, though the very idea of his flirting with *her* was hard to accept. But of course he was a Frenchman, and saying pretty and flattering things to a woman no doubt came to him naturally. Only not, surely, to Brianna Gaze! That was something very new.

She looked at him warily, through her lashes now, knowing that his particular brand of good looks—those highish cheekbones, the compelling blueness of his eyes, the—the *adventurous* curve of his mouth—stirred her in some way.

Who was that other woman? she longed to ask him.

'Well,' he said into the silence that had become somehow tense, 'if it's untrue that you want to leave us, then of course you must stay. I'd like to know why Isabelle was so positive, that's all.' His eyebrows rose interrogatively. 'You have no idea?'

Her tongue touched her top lip nervously. 'No,' she said definitely, deciding against admitting that Isabelle appeared suddenly to have had enough of her. 'Perhaps she thinks I've been here long enough. I'm an outsider, I suppose—not really part of the family. It's always a strain having a house guest for too long.'

'I see.' He looked at her narrowly. 'In that case, Isabelle had better go to Dijon as well as Marie-Claude.'

Brianna stared at him in dismay. That would mean she would be almost alone with him, and she didn't know that she could cope with *that*!

Before she could protest, Isabelle herself came into the living room. She had changed out of the dress she had been wearing earlier and was now looking very pretty in a long cotton skirt and a clinging, sleeveless white top that showed off both her figure and the lovely tan of her shoulders. She had obviously spent some time making up her eyes, and brushing her golden-blonde hair free of its braids, so that her appearance was totally and seductively feminine. She sent Brianna a baleful look that seemed to ask, 'What have you been telling Philippe about me?'

'You were wrong about your sister wanting to go back to England,' Philippe said, without beating about the bush. 'On the contrary, she wishes to stay here. If it's a matter of your resenting her presence here, then the best thing will be for you to leave for Dijon in two days' time, and then we shall all be happy.'

'*Comment?*' Isabelle's cheeks went red and her black eyes smouldered. 'Oh no, Philippe! I shouldn't be happy at all. I've had too much already of the sickly smell of Jean-Christian's bottle and the sound of Olympe's little voice asking this and that all day long. If Brianna's been telling tales about me—we had a little argument, that's all. It was nothing. It's natural when you see too much of each other, but I'm willing to forget it.' She sent Brianna a saucy glance that seemed to put all the blame on her sister. 'I'm sure she's longing to go back to England really. She's trying to be polite. But her boy-friend writes her such long letters——'

'That's enough,' Philippe interrupted. 'The point is, I'm not going to harbour a pair of quarrelsome girls under my roof. If you haven't enough to keep you occupied here, you'll be getting into more mischief. I think it will be best for you to go to Dijon.'

A frantic look came into Isabelle's eyes and she all but stamped her foot as she exclaimed like a furious and spoilt child. 'I shan't go, Philippe! If you send me away you'll be sorry——'

'Oh, don't threaten me, Isabelle.' He turned away and made for the door.

Isabelle burst into tears, and though Philippe had his back to her he could hardly fail to hear the loud sob she gave. 'Poor child!' was Brianna's instant reaction, though she was at a loss to understand Isabelle's intensity. She remembered uneasily Philippe saying the girl could turn on the tears at will—and Richard's remark that she was a dangerous and determined flirt. She didn't know whether to comfort Isabelle or to ignore her sobs as Philippe was doing, but Isabelle wasn't interested in her one way or the other, and she began to run after Philippe, exclaiming tearfully, 'I'll work at my English, Philippe—I promise. I'll be good—really I will. Only please let me stay here!'

Despite everything, Brianna hoped he would. The thought of being alone with him here was too unnerving, somehow, and in her heart, she knew she was beginning to be too much aware of his attractions. And there was no future in that!

CHAPTER EIGHT

PHILIPPE did not relent, and all next day Isabelle was sullen and disagreeable. She had been told to pack her clothes, but Brianna knew she hadn't done so, and she was behaving in much the same way as Brianna herself had behaved in Paris when she was a year or so younger than Isabelle was now. She ate nothing, and she ignored all efforts to talk her back into a better humour.

At the lunch table, Marie-Claude finally gave up and said severely, 'You could enjoy yourself in Dijon if you wanted to, Isabelle. Micheline won't expect you to look after the children now she's back, and there'll be lots of interesting things to do. But of course, if you've made up your mind to sulk, no one will be bothered with you.'

Isabelle pulled a hideously rude face, which caused Olympe to stare at her round-eyed.

'I don't want to do interesting things. I like it here.' She sent her sister an accusing glance. 'It's all your fault, Brianna. Now I know why everyone always called you a troublemaker.'

'Pay no attention to her,' Marie-Claude said uncomfortably, as Isabelle, leaving her food untouched, stalked out of the living room. 'She's at a difficult age, neither one thing or the other. We've grown accustomed to taking her hysterics and tantrums with a grain of salt. She'll get over it soon, and once she gets to Dijon she'll have a wonderful time flirting with every young man she meets. That's what she likes, these days,' she added, as if she herself was well past the stage of flirting.

'Girls become conscious of their sex far too early these

days,' Tante Agathe said disapprovingly. 'That's all that's the matter with Isabelle. She's making herself sick with her silly daydreams. Philippe is quite right to send her away. It's not healthy.'

Brianna, finishing her meal, puzzled over what Tante Agathe had said. Did she mean Isabelle was indulging in daydreams about Emile Dupont? Brianna was quite positive she could have seen no more of him since the day she went mushrooming with him. Strangely, she felt more than a little sorry for Isabelle, and as well she was growing more and more nervous at the thought of being left alone with Philippe. It would be easier if she too were to go to Dijon, but when last night Isabelle had suggested to Philippe that she should stay here with Tante Agnes and Brianna should go to Dijon, he dismissed the idea at once.

'Brianna is not going to be pushed around from one place to another. She is very welcome to stay here.' He had looked at Brianna as he spoke, and her cheeks had burned as she met his eyes and discovered with renewed intensity what they could do to her. If a woman's eyes could make daring statements, then so could a man's. And she didn't believe the messages Philippe's eyes seemed to be sending her, because she knew his heart was engaged elsewhere—with some mysterious woman who was as elusive as a will-o'-the-wisp.

During the afternoon, Richard arrived with the painting for Brianna, and this time it was Marie-Claude who swiftly withdrew, leaving them alone in the garden. Brianna admired the painting, but she felt decidedly doubtful about accepting it as a gift. However, her protests were ignored, and she finally gave in and admitted herself delighted.

'You'll remember France when you're back in England, looking at my sunflowers,' Richard said. 'And you'll remember me.'

'Yes.' She said it with an ache in her heart. She'd remember many things, many people, when she was back in England—she'd remember Philippe—— 'I suppose you'd like to see Marie-Claude,' she said after a moment. 'You know she's going to Dijon tomorrow?'

'Yes. I couldn't persuade her to change her mind. I've been tipped out of my grandmother's house, by the way. I'm now staying at the *auberge* in the square. Grand'mère no longer loves me even a little,' he added with a wry grimace. 'In fact, she holds me entirely responsible for the break up between Marie-Claude and Louis. She'd never believe it if I told her I did no more than look at Marie-Claude when she used to come to Les Charmes to see my cousin. Ah well, such is life. And by the way, *you're* in Grand'mère's bad books too.'

'Me? Why?'

'Oh, she's got it into her head you came to France with the specific purpose of nabbing Philippe d'Hellier, and she'd marked him down for Bertine. A little of the d'Hellier money would be very useful in effecting repairs and renovations to the manor house, and Grand'mère regards Philippe as a man of taste to whom such a project would definitely appeal.'

Brianna's cheeks were burning. 'But—but what can she possibly have against me?'

'I wouldn't have a clue. If she'd seen what I saw that day at the luncheon, she'd be gunning for your sister, not for you. I never saw such blatant provocation from a kid of sixteen in all my life. It's a wonder Philippe doesn't nip it in the bud—but perhaps he's interested.'

'What?' Brianna's colour was brighter than ever. 'You have a nasty mind, Richard. I told you before—Isabelle was just tormenting Philippe.'

'Like fun,' Richard said, then added contritely, 'I'm sorry. You're all up in arms for the honour of your sister, aren't you? So I'll say no more. Anyhow, I wanted to tell you what I've decided to do. I'll go to Dijon myself in a day or two. Nothing venture, nothing win, and Marie-Claude hasn't actually discouraged me. Though I'm beginning to think all this stuff one hears about sexy French girls has no foundation. I haven't even managed to kiss Marie-Claude yet, but I'm mad about her just the same.'

'Well, Rome wasn't built in a day,' Brianna said brightly, and went inside in search of Marie-Claude. She put her painting in a prominent place in the living room, then started up the stairs to her room. But before she reached it, she saw Isabelle from the landing midway up the stairs. Her sister was emerging hurriedly from the garage, wheeling a bicycle. Either she was going to Les Fleurons to meet Philippe or she was going to the farm to meet Emile, Brianna decided, and with the mood Isabelle was in, she wasn't going to take any chances. She flew down the stairs again, went through the front door, and caught Isabelle just as she was opening the great gate that gave on to the narrow street.

'Where are you off to, Isabelle?'

Isabelle didn't even pretend. 'I'm going out to the farm. Why?' she said aggressively.

'That's a question I should ask you. Are you looking for trouble? You know what Philippe said, and you know what Emile is like.'

'*What*'s he like? What do *you* know about him?' Isabelle said defiantly.

'*Isabelle!*' Brianna gripped the handlebar of the bicycle as if she intended forcibly to stop her sister from going. 'You know what he's like—you must. It's—it's obvious. You have only to talk to him. He'll—take advantage of you if he thinks you're encouraging him.'

Isabelle shrugged. 'I don't mind if he kisses me. It's exciting. And if I don't like it, I can run away. At least he doesn't treat me as if I were a child.'

'But you are a child,' Brianna said despairingly, and added, when Isabelle sent her a look of fury, 'In a lot of ways, anyhow. Have you considered what might happen if you couldn't run away? You're really going to be hurt.'

'Hurt? Don't you think I've been hurt already, with Philippe sending me away to Dijon when all I want is to stay here? If it weren't for you it would never have happened.'

Brianna heard her with growing impatience. It struck her that Isabelle was either reckless and irresponsible, or else she was totally unaware that she could be asking for a very nasty experience. She said sharply, 'Well, it won't do anyone any good if you run off and have an—an unsavoury adventure with Emile Dupont.'

'It will show Philippe I'm an adult.'

'It will show Philippe you're a fool. Besides, he told you before, if you don't do as he says he won't allow you to come here any more.'

Isabelle leaned against the gatepost and looked at her sister with a passionate intensity.

'I've been doing what he says. That's exactly what I *have* been doing. But he's still sending me away. I don't want to go to Dijon. If he makes me go, then he'll be sorry. I'm going to do something to deserve it. That's logical, isn't it? But you want me to go away, don't you? You're in love with Philippe, aren't you?'

Brianna stared at her sister, the colour slowly ebbing from her cheeks. 'Of course I'm not,' she said faintly, yet even as she said the words, she knew how blatantly untrue they were. If she wasn't *quite* in love with Philippe, she was perilously near it. It needed only for him to take her in his arms one more time and she would be lost. And that was why she was so afraid to be alone with him. It was why she *didn't* want Isabelle to go.

She told her sister with an agitation she hoped was not

apparent, 'I don't know why you should imagine such a thing. Besides, you told me he's in love with someone else.'

A strange look came into Isabelle's eyes. 'So he is—and don't you forget it, Brianna! He'll marry her in a year or two, though it's not possible yet.'

'Why not?' Brianna breathed out the question despite herself.

'Oh, I'm not going to tell you any more. Philippe says I must learn to hold my tongue. But you see, it's no use your setting your cap at him.'

'I know that,' said Brianna slowly, then brought her mind back to the present situation. 'Look, Isabelle. Please don't go to Dupont's. You really mustn't. It would be crazy. I promise I'll ask Philippe to let you stay—not to send you to Dijon.'

'Why should he take any notice of you?' Isabelle sounded scornful.

'Perhaps he won't. But at least I can try. You know it won't do you the least good to disobey him this way.'

Isabelle shrugged. 'I don't care any more. What's the use, if I'm to go? I might as well make it worth while.' She sounded more stubborn than ever, and she looked like a sulky child, her brows lowered, her mouth drooping. Then she said cautiously, 'Well, all right. Ask Philippe. And if he says no, I'll make you both sorry for it.'

Brianna sighed. Such melodrama! But she wouldn't put it past Isabelle to carry out her threat. However, it was something that she had persuaded her to be sensible now, and a few seconds later, after Isabelle had gone back to the house, it was Brianna who mounted the bicycle and set off in the direction of Les Fleurons.

She had never been to Philippe's vineyards, but she knew the direction and she pedalled along the road steadily, trying not to think back to that moment when Isabelle had accused, 'You're in love with him,' and she had realised how close to the truth it was. It was totally incomprehensible, because she had disliked him so much. Or perhaps, she amended that thought as she whirred along the dirt road, perhaps she had only imagined she disliked him. He was associated in her mind with an unpleasant time of her life, and she saw him as one of her enemies. In fact, she had started by judging him on the past just as she had condemned him for doing to her.

It was strange to recall how she had assured Peter Arden that she didn't want to impress Philippe d'Hellier, and that the last thing she would do would be to fall in love with a Frenchman. Yet even then—even then, in some perverse way, she knew she had been attracted to him. There had been a curious recognition in her heart when he had appeared at her door in Canterbury after an interval of seven years. She had been like the Sleeping Beauty of whom she had been reading to Olympe, she reflected fancifully, waiting for the prince to waken her. With a kiss. And that, perhaps, was how it had happened. If he had never kissed her, she would never have been stirred by him. He shouldn't have done it, of course, and she hoped he didn't know how she felt, because it wasn't fair. Not when there was someone else ...

She suddenly realised that a car was coming towards her, and since the road was so narrow, she slowed down and dismounted from her bicycle. It was only then, as she drew away to the side of the road, her feet among the tangled grasses and the scarlet of the poppies, that she realised it was Philippe's Citroën.

He pulled up level with her and put his head out of the window.

'Is there something wrong at home?'

'No.' She stared at him bemusedly, her senses overwhelmed by the sight of him. Her eyes devoured the familiar lines of his face, the thickness of his hair, the curve of his lips, then returned to the dazzling blue depths of his eyes, and she almost forgot why she was here. When she remembered, she thought she must be mad. There had been no need to cycle out here, as if to plead Isabelle's cause were a matter of great urgency. She could as well have waited till he came home. Now she felt embarrassed, not only because of that, but because there was really no earthly reason why he should alter his plans to please her.

'Well, were you looking for me?' he quizzed, after a moment. 'Or are you just out for some exercise? If it's the latter, then carry on, don't let me hold you up.'

Brianna moistened her lips nervously. 'I—I did hope to see you. I've been thinking, Philippe—and there's—there's something I want to ask you.'

'Yes? Then suppose we put your bicycle in the boot and you sit down in the car and tell me all about it. It must be something important that it can't wait till I return home,' he added dryly, as he climbed out of the car and opened the boot.

Brianna made no answer but got into the front seat and waited for him with a feeling of trepidation. Her mind went back of its own accord to the last time she had been in his car—and he had kissed her with such unexpected passion and then remarked that kissing in cars was not his scene. Well, at least there was hardly likely to be a repetition of it today.

He got into the car, slammed the door, and lit a cigarette. 'Now what's it all about?' he asked tersely. 'I hope you and Isabelle haven't been quarrelling again.' He paused and looked at her, his eyebrows raised. Then as several seconds passed and she hadn't found a way to say what she wanted, he asked ironically, 'Have you decided you want to go back to England after all, and don't know how to break it to me?'

Her face flamed. 'No, it's not that. It's about Isabelle.

I—I wish you wouldn't make her go to Dijon. She doesn't *want* to go, and after all, she's my sister and we've seen so little of each other. It's not really fair of you to part us unnecessarily. Soon she'll go back to school, and besides, I don't expect to stay very long in Paris with Maman.'

'Why not?' he interrupted.

She spread her hands. 'I just have that feeling. I'm too— old to fit into my mother's life now. You said yourself it was too late. Besides, I disrupted her life before, if you re-member. That was why you advised your father to send me away. He and I are still strangers to each other. There's no reason why he should be delighted to have me around the place.'

'If your mother wants you, then I'm sure that will be suf-ficient reason for him, especially when she's been ill.'

'Yes, well, we'll see ... But that was what I wanted to ask you, anyhow. To let Isabelle stay.'

'Is it what you really want? Or has Isabelle been turning on the tears and impressing you with her tantrums?'

'No. I'd like her to stay.'

'Are you afraid of being left alone with me?' he asked bluntly, his gaze intent and unavoidable.

Her pulses quickened guiltily. 'I'm more likely to be bored than afraid.'

His mouth curled up at one corner. '*Non pas.* I think you are afraid.' He stubbed out his cigarette and tossed it through the window, then turned towards her. 'You're even frightened of being alone with me now, *ma petite.* What do you think is going to happen? Do you fear I might make love to you?'

'No.' Her voice was husky and she glanced up at him and smiled shakily. 'I know you don't like kissing in cars.'

'*C'est vrai,*' he said mockingly. 'I've grown beyond it. But of course, when there's no alternative there's nothing to be done about it, is there?'

She edged away from him slightly, the colour rising in her cheeks. 'That's nothing to do with the point, anyhow. About Isabelle——'

'Oh, let Isabelle stay, then, if you want it so much,' he said dismissively, and reaching out he pulled her to him, holding her just far enough away to enable him to look into her eyes in comfort. 'Things have changed between us, haven't they, *mignonne*? We were very wary of each other when we met again, but now we've both stopped threshing around and showing our worst side, we begin to see the good in each other.'

Brianna swallowed on a dry throat. Was this just the— the French way of making peace at the end of a senseless feud? It wasn't, she soon discovered, because Philippe drew her closer with a swift determination and lowered his head to lay his mouth gently against hers, then slowly and tantalisingly to brush his lips against the softness of her own. She caught her breath and stayed passive, and then with sudden urgency he took her mouth in a kiss of passion that at first shocked her and then filled her with an indescribable feeling of ecstasy. Her whole consciousness was centred acutely in the meeting and merging of their mouths. It was a highly erotic sensation, something she had never experienced before—a purely sensual delight that didn't satisfy but left her with an aching hunger for something more.

When his lips left hers he raised his head a little and their eyes met for a long moment. She was aware that her fingers were caressing the back of his neck under the warmth of his hair, and that one of his hands had moved slowly and with a delicate sensuousness down her spine to its very base. He said her name in a husky voice that thrilled her unutterably——

'Brianna——'

'Philippe,' she murmured back, half in a trance, and as

she said it she began to return to her senses. This was
crazy—meaningless. And yet—and yet it was not. It was
real, so real. All Isabelle's talk of another girl meant nothing. The other girl mattered as little as Albertine Moreau.
She was the girl in Philippe's arms, the one he was murmuring to, the one he was caressing.

She submitted willingly when he kissed her again, and
moved away with reluctance when he said at last, 'We'd
better be on our way, *chérie*, before this gets the better of
us ...'

Isabelle was neither grateful nor delighted when he told her
later, at the dinner table, that she could stay on in Huchet-
les-Anges. 'To please your sister—so see you behave yourself.'

She tossed her head. 'You talk to me as though I were
ten years old,' she said haughtily.

Philippe went to the vineyards next day, but returned
home before lunch, as it was then that Paul and Micheline
were expected. Brianna felt herself something of an outsider at the family reunion, though Paul greeted her with
polite friendliness, and Micheline, who possibly knew very
little about her except that she was Isabelle's sister, thanked
her warmly for helping with the children.

She was invited later to go to Dijon, and Isabelle for one
was enthusiastic.

'Oh, you must go, Brianna,' she enthused. 'You said you
would like to.'

Brianna, who hadn't said any such thing, felt embarrassed. She didn't want to go and now they were all—
Marie-Claude, Paul, Isabelle, and even Tante Agathe—
agreeing with Micheline that it was a wonderful idea. In the
midst of the clamour of excited French voices, with everyone talking at once, she turned helplessly to Philippe. If
he said, 'Go', then she knew she would have to go, and

perhaps, in that case, she wouldn't want to stay. But miraculously, Philippe said no.

'Isabelle and Brianna both wish to stay here. After all, they're sisters. And there will be other times. Perhaps after a short while in Paris, Brianna might like to visit Dijon, if the invitation still holds.'

The hubbub subsided, Philippe had spoken, and in no time it seemed as if the idea had never come up. It was completely forgotten—and Brianna as well—as the children once again took the centre of the stage, and Philippe and Paul conducted an animated discussion on the state of the wine industry in Burgundy. Then at last the family from Dijon, plus Marie-Claude, all bundled into the car and drove off.

Three days of summer rain followed immediately upon their departure, and during those three days Philippe stayed out at the vineyards, not even coming home at night. Brianna reflected that after all, she need not have been afraid of being alone with him ...

'It's a worrying time,' Tante Agathe said, while the two sisters stayed disconsolately in the house, playing Scrabble or listening to tapes that belonged to Philippe and didn't please Isabelle, who grumbled that they were all classical. 'Such rain can undo the whole year's work and ruin the harvest. It's to be hoped it doesn't continue much longer,' she concluded as she glanced out the windows at the garden obscured by rain.

Brianna tried to persuade herself she was glad to be free of Philippe's disturbing presence, but it wasn't true. She longed to see him again, and the evenings seemed interminable when he wasn't there.

On the fourth day the sun shone again, and the earth steamed in a renewed burst of summer heat. Tante Agathe, aided by Violette, worked in the house and Isabelle decided to spend the morning beautifying herself, while Brianna walked into the village to do the shopping. She had completed her purchases and was lingering in the square, wondering if she'd call at the *auberge* to enquire if Richard was still there, when she unexpectedly came face to face with Madame Hubert-Benoise. She felt herself curl up inside under the haughty old lady's cold regard.

'*Bonjour, madame*,' she murmured politely, and added the customary French enquiry, '*Ça va?*'

The other woman ignored her greeting. 'So you are still here, *mademoiselle*,' she almost hissed out. 'I wonder you have the temerity to address me since you have deliberately meddled in plans that were made with such care and thought for the people concerned. But believe me, Philippe will soon tire of an English girl.'

'I beg your pardon,' Brianna said with freezing politeness, though inwardly she was positively tied up in knots with indignation. 'I'm afraid I don't know what you're talking about. I'm not to blame if your plans haven't succeeded.' She paused and glanced at the *auberge*. 'Perhaps you can tell me if Richard Hazelwood is still in Huchet-les-Anges?'

'I can tell you nothing. I have washed my hands of my English grandson. He's as meddlesome as you are. I wish you good day.' And with that, she turned abruptly and walked away.

Brianna drew a deep breath. She was not guilty of deliberately stealing Philippe's affections from Bertine Moreau, and she couldn't for the life of her imagine how Madame Hubert-Benoise had got such a thing in her head. There was no one apart from Philippe who knew there was anything between them. Yet after all, what *was* there between them? Exactly nothing—except that he had kissed her on three separate occasions. That was all.

All? In her heart of hearts she couldn't see it that way. That last time, she had felt so close to him, not only to his

physical being but to his spirit. She had felt her own spirit
go out to him to make a deep and meaningful contact. Yet
she was acutely aware that while she felt all this, while she
was rapidly losing her heart to him, she might mean little
or nothing to him. He was an enigma. He had disclaimed
ever having an interest in Bertine, but there was still that
other mysterious woman of whom Isabelle would tell her so
little. Of her he had said nothing, and neither had Tante
Agathe nor Marie-Claude.

It had been subtly wounding to he condemned in so
outright a fashion by Madame Hubert-Benoise, but presently Brianna had regained her composure and went into
the *auberge*.

There she discovered that Richard had not yet left, and
he came downstairs to the small vestibule where she waited
and greeted her warmly.

'I was packing up. Now the rain is over, I'm off to Dijon
to try my fortune. I intended calling in to say goodbye before I took off, of course. How's every little thing?'

She shrugged. 'Oh—quiet. There's only Isabelle and myself left now, apart from Tante Agathe. Philippe hasn't been
home for a few days. Apparently the rain may have en-
dangered the harvest. Have you heard from Marie-Claude?'

'Not a word. I have no idea what sort of reception's in
store for me. But I'm hopeful.'

'I think you should be,' Brianna said sympathetically.

They talked for a little while longer, then said goodbye
and she left. As she walked slowly back along the narrow
street to Philippe's house, it seemed to her that everything
was changing very rapidly. In no time, Maman would return to Paris and it would be time for her to leave. Would
Philippe care? She had no idea. He might even be glad to
be rid of her.

He came home that night, and immediately the whole
feel of the house seemed to alter. Isabelle was full of

vivacity and had never looked prettier. Of course, she had spent half the day prettying herself up, and she was determined to get some sort of a compliment from Philippe, drawing his attention to her new hairstyle, the bracelet he had given her last Christmas, her form-fitting blouse.

'You look very charming, *ma chère*,' he told her briefly, then immediately began to talk to Tante Agathe about the harvest, and to assure her that the rain had done no damage to the greater part of his vines. Later, over coffee, he suggested genially to Brianna that she might like to visit Les Fleurons with him next day.

'*Et moi aussi*, Philippe!' Isabelle interposed poutingly before he had even finished speaking.

'You? You'd be bored, little one,' Philippe said lightly. 'You've been to the vineyards a hundred times. It will be a new experience for Brianna.'

'Oh, let her come, Philippe,' pleaded Brianna, disturbed by the mutinous expression that had passed over her sister's pretty face. 'We've both been shut up in the house for three days——'

He agreed with a shrug, and the next day the three of them departed in the Citroën for the vineyards.

There, Brianna met Edouard Meunier, Philippe's cellarmaster, a man of fifty or so, who lived with his wife in a handsome stone house on the property. After she had been conducted to see the vine-covered slopes where the fruit among the leaves was already beginning to swell, Philippe took her across the big cobbled court to the *chai*, which they entered through double doors. It was a vast room, two stories high, and here he showed her the great vats where after the harvest the mash would be put to ferment for three or four days before it was stirred and pumped into the screw press that stood to one side. As well, she saw the *égrappoir*, a machine for separating the stems from the grapes. She found it all deeply interesting, but not so

Isabelle, who, as Philippe had predicted, was plainly bored
and wandered round the stone room restlessly. Brianna
made one or two efforts to draw her attention to what
Philippe was saying, but she exclaimed with a toss of her
head, 'Oh, I'm not here to see the sights like you, Brianna.
I know all about how Philippe makes his wines—I could
have explained it all to you and saved him the *ennui*.'

Philippe took no notice and continued to give his attention to Brianna.

When they went outside again, Isabelle strolled off in the
direction of the slopes where men in blue jackets and black
berets, reminding Brianna of the Duponts, were working in
the sun. Philippe let her go.

'Come, I'll show you the *caves*,' he told Brianna. 'And
you must taste some of my wines.'

She hesitated, looking worriedly after her sister. 'But
Isabelle—won't she want to come?'

'You've already seen that she's bored with our company.
She'll find it a great deal more amusing to—chat up some
of the young men,' he said, using the English expression
with a crooked smile. 'She'll be quite safe, so don't feel
alarmed. There's not an Emile Dupont at Les Fleurons.
Let her do as she pleases.'

Brianna gave in.

The cellars were beneath the *chai*, and they were entered
by a separate door that led down a flight of old stone steps.
It was cool and dark there, and Philippe switched on a low-
powered light, then took a long glass pipette from its hook
on the wall.

'Get yourself a glass, Brianna,' he said, nodding towards
a row of gleaming crystal goblets on a shelf along the wall.
She did as he said, staring round her at the rows of great
casks with mysterious letters and numbers written on them.
Philippe tapped one of them with his knuckles. 'One day
this will be a wine to please some of the most discriminat-

ing palates in Europe,' he remarked. 'But I shan't distress your digestive system by asking you to swallow it down while it's green.' Using a crowbar, he gently removed the bung from the barrel, then inserted the pipette, tapping the end of it until it was full. He put a little of the wine into Brianna's goblet, and some into a glass for himself, and Brianna admired its rich red colour, displayed to its full advantage by the cut glass. Imitating Philippe, she smelled it, and took a sip. But while Philippe, after tasting it, spat it out on the floor, she swallowed down her mouthful and took another.

She hesitated to say it was good—she was no connoisseur, and all too conscious that her opinion was worthless, but she was enjoying the delicate flavour, the faintly flowery perfume, the thrill of it all.

'Yes, it will be a good wine,' he said quizzically, watching the expressions that flitted across her face. 'A little longer in the cask, then more ageing in the bottle, and it will be a wine ready to present to the world, bearing the Les Fleurons label. But don't drink any more,' he warned smilingly. 'A green wine doesn't lie easily on the stomach, and at lunch you shall taste something worthy of these vineyards. For I am out to impress you, *chérie*!'

They tasted three more wines—and this time she spat her tasting out on the earth floor as he had done—and then he put an arm around her shoulders and they made their way back up the stairs towards daylight and the brilliance of the sunshine.

Brianna glanced around at once for Isabelle, whom she could not see.

'Shall we go and look for Isabelle?' she said anxiously. 'She must be feeling a little neglected.'

'Oh, I'm not going to make a fuss over the child,' he said rather sharply. 'She's all right. Now come along—Madame Meunier will have a meal ready for us. Isabelle will come, once the men go to lunch. She's not going to stay sulking out of sight for long.'

They walked together towards the house, his arm still around her, and she said, her head bent, 'You're trying to make her regret she didn't go to Dijon, aren't you?'

'Perhaps I am. She should have gone. You and I can amuse ourselves very well without her, don't you agree?'

Brianna looked up into his face and felt a shock go through her as she met his eyes. It would be so easy to persuade herself he was madly in love with her! She had a strong and intoxicating feeling that he would like to take her in his arms here and now and kiss the breath out of her. The very thought was shattering to her composure, because she knew she longed for it to happen, and she glanced away from him hastily.

'You've been reading my mind, Brianna,' he murmured, drawing her closer to his side. 'I'm beginning to feel I can't live without you. I knew it quite certainly those four long days I deliberately exiled myself from you. I don't know that I can allow you to go away to Paris—not for more than a week or so, at any rate. And then on the strict understanding that you come straight back here to me.'

They reached the door of the house as he finished speaking, and already Madame Meunier was hurrying forward to greet them, a smile of welcome on her face. Brianna felt so tightly tensed up it required an effort to smile back as Philippe introduced her. It was agony to have their conversation—if it could be called that—cut off so abruptly and completely before she could discover where it was leading, and whether or not she was imagining things. How serious had Philippe been? she wondered. She was sure that, if he had been English, she would have known if he was merely flirting, but because he was French, she was right out of her depth.

Meanwhile, she must at least pretend to take an intelli-

gent interest in what was happening, as Madame Meunier
conducted them to the dining room, and her husband
joined them and asked her a polite question about what she
had been seeing. They were given their places at the white-
clothed table, and Philippe was just about to seat himself
when Isabelle appeared. Brianna had rather expected her to
be sulking, but she did no such thing. She was flushed and
jaunty, and didn't bother to apologise as she took the chair
Monsieur Meunier held for her.

The meal began, the conversation was all to do with the
vineyard, but soon Isabelle, who had drunk thirstily some
of the red wine that was poured to accompany the beef
casserole, began to hold the floor, just as she had done at a
previous lunch party. She concentrated on Philippe, demanding his attention, and chattered on about how she had
just now, in the vineyard, persuaded a certain Pierre to let
her use his *serpette* to trim a few leaves off the vines.

'How sharp it was, Philippe!—dangerously so. That
funny little hooked blade! Pierre said the handle was made
from a piece of vine root.'

Brianna ate her dinner, enjoyed the wine, and wondered about Isabelle ...

Her sister returned to the subject of Pierre later when
they were driving home to Huchet-les-Anges.

'Pierre says he's often seen me in the village. I know
which is his house, because he described it to me. He didn't
guess for a moment that I'm still at school—he thought I
was eighteen at least! You don't mind my making friends
with him, Philippe? Yet you mind so much about Emile.
Why? Is it because he kissed me?'

Philippe said nothing at all, and glancing at him somewhat surprised, Brianna saw with a slight shock that he was
simply not listening to Isabelle. She suspected he hadn't
heard a word her sister had said. What was it that was so
engrossing him? Was he thinking of—of her? She turned

towards Isabelle, feeling curiously guilty, and discovered a look of frustration and anger behind her girlish animation. Poor Isabelle! What was she looking for? Richard had said she wanted to be rid of Bertine. Did she now want to be rid of Brianna? And if so, why?

She didn't really have to look far for an answer. It must be because she suspected Philippe of falling in love with her, Brianna. Yet why shouldn't Philippe be free to love where he chose? Did Isabelle know something specific about that other girl that she was so determined he should not become involved with anyone else? Or was she simply a very possessive little sister?

CHAPTER NINE

BRIANNA forgot her concern over Isabelle when after dinner that night Philippe, who had said nothing of a private nature to her since they returned home, invited her to take a walk in the garden with him.

'We have certain things to discuss,' he told Tante Agathe, who nodded as though she understood perfectly. What did she think they were going to talk about? Brianna wondered, her heart beating rapidly. True, there had been a letter waiting them when they came home setting the date of Maman's return—five days ahead. So perhaps she thought it was something to do with that. And perhaps—perhaps it was ...

Isabelle had run upstairs to fetch a magazine that had some dress designs she was interested in—she had been talking clothes and hair styles all the evening, with a feverish intensity. As Brianna went back through the house with Philippe—they used the salon in the evenings, now that the children had gone—she hoped desperately that Isabelle wouldn't come downstairs again too quickly and spoil their chance of a private conversation. She had had sufficient time by now to think of those moments with Philippe when he had said he couldn't live without her—that he wanted her to come back here to him after she had spent a little time in Paris with her mother. She knew that she felt exactly the same way about him. It was strange how it had happened, seeing she had started out with the feeling she was going to find it impossible to like him. Perhaps it was a combination of the proximity that Madame Hubert-Benoise had mentioned, and the peculiar alchemy of the human body. Physical contact with him had taught her that she wanted him, quite simply. Certainly no vines had been planted and lovingly tended. No one had watched jealously over the shooting of sprouts. This was a wild and wilful burgeoning, and as for the vintage——

She broke off her somewhat fanciful train of thought and glanced up at Philippe as they entered the garden together.

'Your heart's thudding, *mignonne*,' he said in a low, slightly amused voice. He had linked his right arm through her left one, and the fact that he could feel the movement of her heart against her rib cage through the stuff of the long simple dress she was wearing made her heart beat still faster. She was certain now that Philippe intended to continue the conversation that he had begun much earlier in the day, and she wanted it more than anything.

They crossed the court and descended the steps in the low balustrade, and from there moved on to the lawn, their footsteps soundless. It was moonlight and the scent of roses and geraniums was laid upon the air with the lightest touch. Beneath the big chestnut tree, the garden chairs and table gleamed whitely, but once they had reached the scented shadows, Philippe drew Brianna silently into his arms and kissed her, long and thrillingly.

'It's a little more satisfactory, isn't it, *chérie*, than kissing in a car,' he said softly after some time. 'We are closer to each other this way, and the contact of our bodies tells us much about our feelings for each other ... Do you know that I love you?'

She caught her breath. 'I don't know why you should,' she murmured.

'*Non?* Some time I'll tell you every little reason why.' He took her face between his hands and looked down at her, his eyes mysterious in the night. '*Et toi, chérie?* You have forgotten your hatred? You've forgiven my lack of understanding—my part in banishing you when I should have made it possible for you to stay?'

She nodded, her eyes wide. 'And you've forgiven my—my quite *un*forgivable stupidity, and refusal to behave in a civilised way?'

'Every single thing,' he said solemnly. 'And the fact that you're English as well,' he added, his lips curving in a smile. 'Though to tell the truth, I find you have a very Gallic fire which assures me that the blood flowing through your veins is not all British. But I neither know nor care what you are, *chérie*—French or English or a maddening mixture of the two. All I know is that you are woman—that for me you have something that no other woman has.'

He kissed her again, but she pulled herself free to say huskily, 'No other woman, Philippe? Are you—are you sure of that?'

He held her away from him. 'Are you thinking of Bertine? Haven't I already told you there was no romance there? It existed only in the brain of Madame Hubert-Benoise. Bertine perhaps was willing to obey her grandmother's wishes, but I make my own decisions. I thought you were already aware of that.'

'Oh, yes, Philippe.' She swallowed and tried again. 'I—I didn't mean Bertine.'

She saw the dark line of his eyebrows shoot up and caught a flash of blue fire from his eyes. 'Then whom did you mean? You can't have been raking through my past——'

'No.' She had no idea how to go on now. How could she tell him that Isabelle insisted there was someone who, for certain reasons, couldn't marry him yet, but who would certainly marry him later?

While she hesitated, he said in a low voice, 'Come here, Brianna. I'll prove to you there's no other woman for me—that you're the one I love and desire——'

His caresses, his kisses, his tenderness, had her soon in a

state of almost hypnotic happiness, and when he let her go and asked softly, 'Have you any doubts left, darling?' she shook her head. She would forget what Isabelle had said, she had no choice. Philippe loved her and she loved him, and there was no room for doubting.

'You'll go to Paris, of course,' he decreed presently. 'Maman will want to have you with her for a little while, and my father will probably be enchanted. He'll completely forget what a little horror you once were and how you put his marriage in jeopardy. But soon you must come back to Huchet-les-Anges. You'll be here in October for the vintage. It will cement our new relationship, our new feelings for each other—and we'll take it from there. Agreed? Or am I proceeding at a pace too fast for you, my little *anglaise*?'

'No, Philippe,' she said, and was amazed at her own meekness. And so was he, because he laughed and remarked, 'I never expected to hear you agree with me about anything so willingly. But don't worry, I'm not mad enough to believe it will continue indefinitely—I wouldn't want that, in any case. I like your spirit ... You have no regrets and reservations about the man you left in England?'

She sighed a little. 'No. Peter and I were good friends, but it hadn't developed into—anything else as far as I was concerned. I've never given him any—encouragement when I wrote.'

'So it wasn't entirely platonic,' he said half mockingly, half jealously. 'Well, when you do go back to England— and I daresay you'll want to do that before we marry— then I shall go with you. Just to make sure.'

His words sent a thrill through her. Before we marry! How incredible it was! She was actually going to do what she had said she'd never do, and marry a Frenchman. But after all, she was half French herself—and only just becoming aware of it.

She was back in his arms when the house door slammed and Isabelle's voice called sharply, 'Are you there, Philippe?'

'My God—that child!' he said under his breath. 'Will she never learn diplomacy?'

Isabelle was looking down at them from the balustrade, and Philippe kept his arm around Brianna as he told her, 'We're coming inside presently, *ma chère*. Make some coffee, will you, and we'll have it together.'

Isabelle didn't answer. She disappeared inside, but when they went indoors she had gone upstairs to bed.

She was moody the next day, moody and uncommunicative, and Brianna knew for sure that it had something to do with Philippe's attentions to her. It put a damper on her own feelings of happiness, and she felt troubled. It was beginning to be plainer than ever that Isabelle was very possessive of Philippe and of course, she had known him so much longer than Brianna had. Brianna didn't know quite how to deal with the situation, and simply tried to behave as if nothing were wrong, but Tante Agathe, who might be aware of what was happening between Brianna and Philippe and equally well might not, was not so tolerant.

'You should have gone to Dijon, *mademoiselle*,' she told Isabelle tartly, as the girl sat silent at the lunch table. There were only the three of them as Philippe had not come home. 'You've been idle too long. Huchet-les-Anges is no place for a young and single girl in the long summer vacation.'

Isabelle raised her black eyes. 'I'm beginning to agree with you, Tante Agathe. But I used to have a good time here in other years, and I was happy this year until Brianna and the children came and Philippe became so disagreeable. Next summer it will be different again, you'll see.'

'Next summer I'll be surprised if Philippe agrees to have you here at all,' Tante Agathe said dryly.

Brianna didn't join in the argument. What *would* next summer bring? she wondered. Would she and Philippe be married by then? It would be a shame if Isabelle couldn't come to stay, and yet it was true that the little village was hardly an exciting place for a girl of sixteen or seventeen. In a way, it was no wonder that Isabelle had diverted herself with Emile Dupont. But by next year, when she was a little more mature, she might well prefer to go to Dijon, or to the gaiety of Nice, where Honorine lived. Well, time would tell.

She was surprised when later that afternoon Isabelle, who had been upstairs in her room, came down to the garden to ask Brianna to go for a walk with her. Brianna was weeding the garden and thinking private thoughts about Philippe, while Tante Agathe sat in the shade doing some crochet work.

Brianna tossed down the little garden trowel at once. It looked as if Isabelle were holding out an olive branch and she was only too glad to accept it.

'I'd love that,' she said with a smile, but her sister's smile in return was wary.

'Then let's go.'

They set out a few minutes later and had soon left the village behind and started up a small road that went up the hillside.

'Where are we going?' Brianna asked her rather uncommunicative sister.

'To the forest. Perhaps we'll find the *source* ... Would you like to see the little *chapelle*?'

'Very much,' Brianna said agreeably, eager to believe that her sister's bout of the sulks had come to an end. But Isabelle was still not inclined to be talkative, which was unlike her, for she was a real chatterbox, and when Brianna asked if it was the source of the little stream called the

Huchet that they would look for, she didn't bother to answer.

By now they had entered the forest, and here the path was so narrow they must walk one behind the other. It was cool and green and shady after the heat of the steep hillside road. Wild raspberries grew by the way and the path was thick with the fallen leaves of many autumns, so that their footsteps made no sound. Brianna listened to the birds, and tried to catch a glimpse of them among the branches, and she gathered for herself an armful of pink and yellow wild flowers to take back to the house. She would put them in the earthenware bowl Marie-Claude used for wildflowers, she decided. They would look attractive on the small landing over the stairway. Philippe liked flowers in the house. Tante Agathe always saw that there were fresh flowers in his study, a room into which Brianna had never ventured, never been invited. There were always flowers on his long narrow desk, she knew—she had seen them through the open door as she passed many times.

She occupied herself happily with her thoughts as she followed her sister, giving up the attempt to make conversation for her few eager questions about the birds, and a species of nut tree she had observed, had brought no response at all from Isabelle.

Soon they left what had been a well defined path to follow one that looked as if it were seldom used. Branches had fallen across it here and there, and the long prickly tendrils of blackberry bushes grasped at their ankles as they passed along. It was a curious sort of path to be following, but Isabelle must surely know where she was going, and finally they broke out into a small clearing on the hillside.

Isabelle stopped and turned to look at her sister.

'This is the *chapelle*. The *source* is somewhere near, if you like to look for it.'

Brianna stared about her fascinated. In the clearing were the ruins of a small and very old chapel that looked as if no one had visited it for a very long time. Clasping her bouquet of wildflowers to her breast, she moved forward, a little awed. From the arched and broken entrance to the tiny chapel, a stone face looked down at her, compassionate still, though the features were almost obliterated by age. Above it were carved the words, '*Sainte Reine, Aidez-nous.*' 'Holy Queen, aid us,' she translated softly. She turned to share her slightly emotional reaction with her sister, but Isabelle was sitting on a fallen log easing the strap of her sandal, and when she looked up, it was to say accusingly,

'Philippe made love to you last night, didn't he?'

Brianna flinched. The meaning Isabelle gave to those bluntly spoken words was unmistakable, and she said rather coldly, 'He kissed me, that's all.'

'Oh, Brianna!' Isabelle raised her head and flicked back her little pigtails from cheeks that were flushed with exertion. 'You don't have to pretend to me, I know all about kissing—I learned from Emile ... Do you know *why* he made love to you?'

Of course she knew why, but Brianna felt distaste, and she said still coldly, 'I don't think I really want to talk about it to you, Isabelle. It's—it's something that's just between Philippe and myself.'

'That's what you think,' Isabelle retorted, her smile malicious. 'And the reason's *not* the one you think, you see. Do you want me to tell you what it's all about?'

Brianna was disconcerted. 'I don't know what you mean.'

'Then listen. Do you know that Maman owns a small portion of the Clos des Anges? No? Well, in case you don't know about *that*, it's the most venerated vineyard in this area. Every *vigneron* in the district would give his eyes to own a portion of the Clos des Anges, because of the prestige. Philippe wants it more than anything. It would make his wines worth a fortune if he could put the name of Clos des Anges on the bottle.'

Brianna frowned. 'I don't know anything about such things,' she said after a moment. 'But in any case, what has it to do with Philippe and me?'

'Oh, don't be stupid. Brianna! Can't you see?' Isabelle jumped up from the log and paced restlessly to the little chapel and back again, then stood confronting her sister. 'The vineyard will be *his* if he marries you—he'll ask Maman to let *you* have it, and he always gets what he wants. Haven't you noticed? He'd have to wait two years to—to gain it through me, the way—the way Maman always planned. But this way, if he pretends he loves *you*, he can have it so much sooner.'

She stopped, and Brianna stared at her aghast, trying to take in the sense of what she had said. Philippe was—pretending to love her so that he could gain possession of a vineyard! She couldn't believe it. Yet what did she know of the machinations that went on in his mind? The implications of it all made her feel sick right through to her heart. Oh, how stupid she had been—how gullible! To believe that he had fallen in love with her—to have responded to his passion as though it were as sincere as her own! And all the time, in that logical French brain of his, he was scheming to use her for mere material gain . . .

She looked unseeingly at Isabelle and whispered, 'It can't be true! I—I don't believe it.'

'It *is* true,' Isabelle said, stony-faced. 'If you marry him you'll find out—you'll be sorry. Has he—has he asked you yet?'

Brianna nodded tragically. 'He—he talked of it last night.'

'You're not to marry him,' Isabelle exclaimed with a touch of hysteria. 'Why don't you go back to England?

That's where you belong. We don't want you here, you've
—you've spoilt everything! It's been a horrible summer
—I'm going to tell Philippe you want to go—you want to
marry Peter Arden. I'll—I'll swear to it. And you'd better
agree. Otherwise you'll be sorry, both of you. I'll make sure
of that!'

Brianna hardly heard her last confused exclamation, and
she was barely aware of it when Isabelle turned away and
began to run off along the forest path as if she were determined to go to Philippe straight away. It scarcely mattered
if she did, Brianna thought, as with a stifled groan she
collapsed on the log where Isabelle had been sitting. She
didn't care what Isabelle told him. Her mind was in a
turmoil and the only thing that seemed clear was that she
would have to leave Huchet-les-Anges. Perhaps she
wouldn't even wait to see Maman—perhaps she'd go
straight to Canterbury where motives were simple and
above board and she knew what was going on.

And what would Philippe do—Philippe who wanted
that valuable little vineyard 'more than anything'?

She found she was staring up at the lovely stone face that
looked back at her with such sweet pity.

Then—oh God! The truth burst on her like a fiery
rocket exploding against a dark sky. Of course! Philippe
would marry Isabelle—as *Maman had planned. Isabelle*
was the other girl—the girl he couldn't marry yet. But
when she was eighteen—yes, he would marry Isabelle then,
Isabelle and the vineyard that would be given to her—so
long as Brianna, interfering English Brianna, who spoilt
everything, was out of the way. And Philippe would love
Isabelle just as much as he was prepared to love Brianna.

'Oh, we are great lovers,' she could hear Madame
Hubert-Benoise saying dryly. 'But love can be cultivated——'

So Philippe had carefully cultivated the love that had

seemed to spring up of its own accord between himself and
Brianna—and she had made it so easy by falling for all
that French charm. She wondered if Madame Hubert-
Benoise knew about Maman's little plot in the Clos des
Anges, if that was why she made sure Brianna knew his
heart was engaged elsewhere. And if that was why she had
said Philippe would soon tire of her, once he had the vineyard . . .

It was a long time before she gathered the strength to
get to her feet again, and then she discovered her face was
wet with tears. She dreaded the thought of going 'home', of
seeing Philippe again, knowing what she knew now. She
hoped desperately that Isabelle would have seen him first,
and told him that she wanted to go back to England to
Peter Arden. If he taxed her with it, she would acquiesce.
It would be easier that way—more quickly ended.

Her tears began to fall once more.

CHAPTER TEN

SHE began to walk stumblingly back along the forest path, blind to its beauties now, knowing that she had left her bouquet of wildflowers in the clearing, but not caring. There was little sense in trying to please Philippe any more.

It took her a long while to get back to the village. Somehow she took the wrong way, and had to retrace her steps several times, until at last, after forcing her way through a tangle of brambles, she found herself on the path that led back to the road.

She was late, but Philippe was not there when she reached the house. There was no one but Tante Agathe in the kitchen, and she was engrossed in making a quiche for the evening meal.

'Is—is no one home, Tante Agathe?'

Tante Agathe glanced up and then her eyes sharpened as she looked at her hard, and Brianna suddenly realised that her battle with the brambles had left her somewhat dishevelled, and that as well her face was stained with tears. She pushed back her hair and said tiredly, 'I lost myself in the forest. I—I wanted to stay and look for the *source*. Is Isabelle upstairs? Did she come home?'

'Yes, *ma chère*, she came home, but she took the bicycle and went out again—to Les Fleurons.' Tante Agathe glanced at the clock. 'She and Philippe should be home any moment now—it's late.'

'Yes. I'll go upstairs and tidy myself up, and then I'll come down and help you with the supper.'

'No, no, there's no need for that. Have a rest, dear child. You look tired out.'

Brianna turned away quickly, for the kind words brought weak tears to her eyes, and for the first time she realised she had become very fond of Philippe's elderly aunt. She could have lived with her quite happily.

Upstairs in her room—the *chambre d'amis*—she stood staring about her vacantly. She had no heart for anything, but she must change, of course, and make herself look presentable. She opened the wardrobe and took down one of the long dresses she had bought in Canterbury with the express purpose of proving to the d'Hellier family that she was sophisticated and smart, even if she was English. Sophisticated! She stared at her white strained face in the mirror and laughed mirthlessly. She was as simple as Bertine, twice as simple as Isabelle—and how well Philippe must know it! She had swallowed his compliments and tender words down whole.

Unable to bear her thoughts, she picked up her brush and began brushing the shine back into her hair. She could hear movements in the upstairs hall. They must be home, Isabelle and Philippe. Her sister would have told him by now that Brianna wanted to go back to her English boy-friend. That would surprise him, and perhaps he would take some convincing. But convince him she would, and then Isabelle would have Philippe to herself. She had wanted that all along—not simply because she was possessive, but because Maman had planned that Philippe should marry her when she was eighteen, and she was determined that no one would take him away from her. And then Brianna had come along and thrown her whole little world into confusion . . .

Someone knocked on the door, and Brianna put down her brush and called, 'Come in.' She expected Isabelle, but it was Philippe who stood in the doorway for what seemed an eternity, saying nothing, but simply looking at her meditatively, his eyes very blue. She looked back at him and felt despair. She loved him—and now that she was not to have him she knew just how much she loved him. Enough even to go ahead with a marriage that was merely a strategic one. Yes, she knew she would marry him even if his love was mere pretence, but she knew too that it was impossible—because of Isabelle—the 'other girl'—her own sister.

'Are you all right?' Philippe asked. 'Tante Agathe wondered if you should have a little brandy.'

Brianna shook her head. 'I'm perfectly all right, thank you, Philippe. Did Isabelle—tell you?' she added, aware that her voice was unnatural.

'Isabelle told me you'd decided to go back to your English friend,' he said matter-of-factly. He came further into the room, shutting the door quietly behind him. 'I don't believe it, of course.'

Brianna's face grew paler than ever. Her lips parted and she stared back at him speechlessly. He took two more long steps and stood close to her—too close—and looked down into her face, his eyes serious. She wished desperately that she could hate him—or at the least feel indifferent to him, but merely to look at him set fire to her senses.

'Your sister has gone too far this time, *ma petite*,' he said. 'I refused to listen to any more of her talk and sent her off home. Tomorrow she goes to Dijon.'

Brianna shook her head vehemently. 'No, Philippe. It's no use sending her to Dijon. She was right, I—I don't want to stay here any longer. I'll go back to England.' She broke off with a gasp of pain as he gripped her by the arms, his hard fingers pressing cruelly into her flesh.

'I think not, little one,' he said between his teeth. 'I'm not as easily fooled at that. Last night you let me make love to you, and we made a mutual confession of our need for each other—not in words, it's true, but in a deeper way.' He shook her slightly. 'What's been going on between you and Isabelle? What stories has she been telling you?'

There was a moment's silence, then she said painfully, 'A story about the Clos des Anges.'

'The Clos des Anges?' He looked completely baffled. 'Dear God, what are you talking about now?' He looked intently into her eyes. 'What are you trying to tell me, Brianna? Come along, let's hear it. Exactly what has Isabelle told you about the Clos des Anges that has suddenly made you decide you must go back to England?'

'Please—please let me go,' she said huskily, unable to bear what his eyes were doing to her. 'You're hurting me——'

'I mean to hurt you.' His voice was savage, but he let her go and she stood rubbing her arms and trembling a little. 'You don't think I'm going to let you run away without fighting for you, do you? I want to know it all.'

'You—you do know it all,' she said. 'I'm the one who was kept in the dark—who knew none of it. You never told me that Maman wanted you and Isabelle to marry. I'd never have——'

'What?' he interrupted, and now his eyes were angry. 'Now listen to me, my little *anglaise*—Maman does *not* want me and Isabelle to marry, and if she did it would make no difference to me or to what I feel for you. Did Isabelle tell you this? and you believed it? What else did she tell you? What's all this about the Clos des Anges? Tell me now—I intend to hear it all if I have to force it out of you!'

Brianna's conviction was wavering, but he was right, he would have to hear it all, and she told him, gritting her teeth, 'I know now that if you marry me, Maman will give me—give *us*—her vineyard in the Clos des Anges. Isabelle said you—you don't really love me at all—it's just the vineyard you want—and you—you don't want to wait for it.' Her voice wavered and broke, and she had to bite her lower lip to stop it from trembling.

'*Chérie*——' His voice was suddenly soft. 'You mustn't believe this, because none of it is true. I think I know your mother better than you do—just as I know Isabelle better. She would never do this thing, not even if I begged her to. The little vineyard has always been promised to Isabelle for her eighteenth birthday, and all the family knows it. It's fair enough, I think. You've been taken care of by your English relatives, Isabelle will be taken care of by the French side of the family ... As for me—I don't want the vineyard, *mignonne*. Did you really think I might? Don't you know I'm content with Les Fleurons and the wines I make there? And if I have both you and Les Fleurons, there is nothing more I can ask of life—except a child, or maybe two.'

As he spoke, he took her into his arms and kissed her gently, and the tears ran slowly down her cheeks.

'But Maman had plans——'

'Maman did not have plans,' he murmured against her hair. 'If you must have the truth, my darling, it's Isabelle who had the plans. She's been hatching them all this long idle summer. She has—what you call a crush—on me. Very intense, but I assure you, no more than a crush. She will recover from it, and to save her dignity, I have pretended not to know.' Brianna looked up briefly into his face, and knew he was telling her the truth. 'I saw it happening and I'd have sent her to Nice except that Maman wanted her two daughters to become friends, so, selfishly, I kept her here. That meant I could have *you* here too, you see, for believe it or not, there was something in you, well hidden behind that angry face you wore, that appealed to me instantly that day in Canterbury. Perhaps even before that—perhaps even that night in Paris when first we met, when you came home from your long ride on the Métro, so pale-faced and wounded and stubborn. So unmanageable, like a little wild

animal with sharp teeth ... Now tell me that you're not
going to run away to England. Admit that you love me as
I love you——'

She moved a little in his arms, remembering Isabelle's
hysteria, her threats to make them sorry. She had wanted to
be friends with her sister, but if she married Philippe, then
did that mean she would make an enemy of her?

'I do love you, Philippe,' she said in despair. 'But I
agreed I would go away, and Isabelle is going to be so
angry if she knows I'm not going. She'll—she'll do something silly, I know she will.'

'I don't think so. She knows already that I won't tolerate
your going away. I made that very plain before I told her to
run off home and stop interfering.'

Brianna looked up at him, wide-eyed. 'Philippe, do you
mean she didn't come home with you?'

'No, of course she didn't, I'd had enough of her and her
silly tales.'

'Then where is she?'

'Sulking in her room,' he suggested without a great deal
of concern.

'But she's not,' Brianna said in alarm. 'Tante Agathe said
she was with you. Oh, Philippe, do you think she went to
the farm instead of coming home? She told me she'd make
us sorry——' She said no more but pushed past him, and
flinging open the door ran along the hall and down the
stairs. It was horrible to think of Isabelle out there at the
farm allowing Emile to maul her—even to——

She wasn't sure what she had it in mind to do—perhaps
to insist that Philippe should drive her out there in the car.
But of course she wouldn't have to insist, she realised as in
the big square hall at the foot of the stairs she stopped to
confront him, for he had been following close behind her.
He was white about the nostrils and she knew he was as
alarmed as she was.

'Get out of my way!' he commanded.

'I'm coming too,' she exclaimed hotly, as Tante Agathe came through from the kitchen to see what all the commotion was about.

At almost the same moment, the back door burst open and Isabelle stood there, her face tragic, her blouse torn, one saucy little pigtail still bobbing, while on the other side of her face her hair fell loosely across her cheek. She stood stock still on finding herself confronted by three staring people, then she burst into tears and with her head down ran into the living room. Brianna felt as if her heart had stopped beating. For an instant she was unable to move, hearing in her mind without wanting to hear it what Emile had said he would like to do to her that evening in the street outside the house. Then, hurriedly, she followed the others into the big room.

Isabelle had thrown herself down on the sofa and was sobbing loudly. Tante Agathe approached and put a gentle hand on her arm, but Philippe took the girl firmly by the shoulder and said sharply, 'Isabelle, calm yourself. Tell us what has happened.'

Isabelle pulled away from him as if she couldn't bear his touch.

'Don't touch me,' she said through her sobs, and shrank against the back of the sofa, her hands over her face. 'I want—I want to go home,' she finished on a childish note, then parted her fingers a little so that one dark eye could look quickly around at the three concerned faces staring at her. Then she began sobbing again.

Tante Agathe looked questioningly at Philippe.

'Emile Dupont,' he said significantly, in an undertone. Then to Isabelle, 'What happened, *ma chère*? Pull yourself together a little and tell us all about it. It will do you good.'

But Isabelle's sobs only increased, and Brianna, imagining something dire, blamed herself bitterly.

'The child will tell me,' said Tante Agathe briskly. 'Please leave us alone.'

Philippe obeyed the order as unquestioningly as did Brianna, but while he went off to his study, she went into the kitchen, carefully closing the door behind her. There, she looked into the oven to see that the quiche was in no danger of burning, then rather helplessly started washing up the basins, the pastry board, and various other kitchen utensils Tante Agathe had been using. 'Poor Isabelle,' she thought. She had looked very chastened, very much as though she had been through an unpalatable experience, but Brianna kept seeing that black eye peeping impudently out at them to see what effect her melodrama was having. Somehow, she reached the conclusion that it couldn't possibly be as bad as she had feared. If something really bad had happened, Isabelle just wouldn't have been capable of that little bit of sauciness.

Some minutes later Tante Agathe opened the kitchen door.

'Your sister's recovered, child,' she told Brianna quietly. 'She ran into Emile at the farm—where she shouldn't have been. She had a little talk with him and then—well, he'd been drinking wine, she said, and he gave her a fright. A kiss or two, and when he demanded something more, the silly girl at least had the sense to run away. That's when her blouse was torn. Well, she won't play tricks like that again in a hurry, though she's enjoying the drama of it all just now.'

Brianna breathed an inward prayer of relief, then rather nervously went back to the living room. Isabelle was sitting on the sofa sipping from a small glass that held brandy, and looking rather important. She had made a remarkable recovery, and despite her slightly swollen eyes she appeared to be well on the way back to being her usual audacious self.

'*Eh bien*, you're welcome to Philippe or Richard or Peter—or any man you like,' she told Brianna after a moment. 'I never want to see another man again—never! And nothing will persuade me to marry, no matter what plans Maman makes. I'll—I'll be a *religieuse*, I think,' she finished with a pious look.

Brianna hid a smile. Isabelle a nun? Never in a million years! But she nodded sympathetically and asked, 'Are you feeling better now, Isabelle?'

'A little. But I shan't want any supper tonight—I've been too upset. I'm going to bed—and tomorrow Tante Agathe will take me to Dijon. She's promised.'

'You'll stay there with Paul and Micheline?'

Isabelle looked thoughtful, then she shook her head. 'No, I'll take the train and go to Nice, to Honorine. That's what I'll do. I'll —I'll get away from everyone ...'

'Well, I suppose we must allow it,' Philippe said when Brianna told him about it in the garden, later on that night. 'There's always a lot going on in Nice, and she'll soon recover from her crush on me there. One or two days and she'll be head over ears in love with someone else—but please heaven there'll be no cause for melodrama when the time comes to go back to Paris and school. As for her being a nun—her mind will soon be changed about that!' He drew Brianna adroitly into his arms and murmured as he brushed his lips against her forehead, 'Have all your doubts about me vanished, *mignonne*?'

'Every one,' she whispered back.

'They didn't last long, then? And you won't be afraid to be alone with me when your sister's gone?'

'I'll be—terrified,' she said with a little laugh. He was pulling her close to him now and his mouth was seeking hers, and she waited, holding her breath, for the delicious moment when their lips would meet. Her Philippe—her wonderful Frenchman ...

Do you have a favorite
Harlequin author?
Then here is an
opportunity you must
not miss!

HARLEQUIN OMNIBUS

Each volume contains
3 full-length compelling
romances by one author.
Almost 600 pages of
the very best in romantic
fiction for only $2.75

A wonderful way to collect
the novels by the Harlequin
writers you love best!

3
GREAT
NOVELS

**Harlequin brings you
a book to cherish ...**

three stories of
love and romance
by one of your
favorite
Harlequin authors ...

JOY
ROMANCE
LOVE

Harlequin Omnibus

THREE love stories in ONE beautiful volume

The joys of being in love...
the wonder of romance...
the happiness that true love brings...

Now yours in the HARLEQUIN OMNIBUS
edition every month wherever
paperbacks are sold.

And there's still *more* love in